WALKERS
C.B. Williams

BOOK ONE OF THE WALKERS TRILOGY

ALCHEMY
RANCH
BOOKS

Published by AlChemy Ranch Books
4409 Lentell Road
Eureka, CA 95503 USA

pubisher@alchemyranchstudios.com
www.alchemyranchstudios.com

Walkers, copyright © 2012 by Cynthia Bryn Williams

ISBN 10: 0988181428
ISBN 13: 978-0-9881814-2-7

Cover art and design by Alan Williams

First AlChemy Ranch Books Edition: August 2012

0987654321

for Sensei Richard Pietrelli

Table of Contents

Chapter 1- Prince Joey

"Ieh!" Kate's wooden training sword cut a perfect diagonal from left to right. She stepped forward, sinking low into her stance, *"Tō!"* The sword cut an opposite diagonal, the street lamp glinting off the polished wood. She paused briefly, then cut again.

Caught in the rhythm, Kate had long since lost track of how many *kesas* she had cut in the chilly pre-dawn of an early March day. Sweat beaded up on her forehead, ran down her back, her front. Her shoulders and forearms burned. She shook the damp bangs from her eyes. Sucking in gulps of air, she stepped, exploding into a *kiai* and a simultaneous cut. She loved the feel of her muscles moving and her breath coming fast and sure. She cut again and again, one cut blending into the other in an endless flow of motion. It made her feel alive. It made her feel strong. In this arena, she could still be good. In this arena, she was still quick.

Kate jumped when the egg timer went off. With a sigh, she picked up the towel she had slung over the back of her parents' car and wiped her face and the back of her neck beneath her long red-gold braid. She stood, momentarily transfixed by the beauty of the pink and yellow dawn, as her breathing returned to normal. The harsh caw of a Jay pulled her from her reverie.

Kate hastily gathered up her training sword and *naginata* and headed towards her front door, towards the shower, towards breakfast, towards school and, it being Wednesday, towards her favorite little person, Joey.

On Wednesdays Kate babysat ten-month-old Joey Sullivan. She really wasn't that keen on kids, let alone babies, but there was something about this little guy that had gotten under her skin. She actually looked forward to the three to four hours she spent with him while his parents went out and "reconnected," as they called it.

First of all, Joey was a beautiful baby—all pink and white, with chubby little legs and midnight curls. And his eyes were an extraordinary shade of green, like beach glass, pale and translucent. Then there was his disposition. Alert, happy, full of life. His smile was contagious. Joey was the proverbial bouncing baby boy, and Kate loved to bask in his sweetness.

And so, to Kate, Wednesdays were perfect days. Her classes were all her favorites, with a study hall right before lunch, which meant she could leave the high school campus for almost two hours because of her good grades. Which meant that she could go home and watch her favorite soap while eating lunch. This particular Wednesday, her best friend Gina was going to join her. And after school she had a private sword lesson with her *Sensei*, followed by a sword class which ended just in time for her to drive over to the Sullivans' home to watch Joey.

* * *

"Come with me to class," Kate begged. "Gina, you'd love it. I know you would! Then we could practice together." She circled her *bokuto* into *mugamae,* the stance of nothingness, and cut a *kurai tachi,* narrowly missing a lamp.

Gina glanced up from where she was sitting in the Johnsons' study putting on her shoes. They were about ready to go back to school for Theatre, their last class of the day. She pushed her glasses back up her nose. "You know, Kate, your mom would have a fit if she saw you swinging that wooden thing in here."

"Good thing she's not here then, huh?" She feigned an attack on one of the trophies lining a bookshelf and scowled. "I wish they'd get rid of all those things. Maybe they like to torture me."

Gina stood up, grabbed her backpack and lightly touched Kate on the shoulder. "They're just proud of you, Kate."

Kate rolled her eyes. "The voice of reason. Yeah, I know. I just don't see the point, and all it does is remind me."

"Well, it *was* your choice," Gina said softly.

Kate sighed. "I know." She looked down at herself, spreading her arms. "This stupid, traitorous body. I *hate* it!"

"You're not too tall for all the events."

Kate flared up. "Gina, have you *ever* seen an Olympic gold medalist my height? No, you have not. And why not? Because tall women aren't for gymnastics. Look at me! I'm five feet, ten inches. That's nearly six feet tall! Why couldn't I have stayed small like you?"

"But, you love gymnastics. Why can't you just do it for, you know, just for the fun of it?"

"Because I've wanted to be in the Olympics for so long that every class I take would just remind me that I can't. It's not fair."

Kate waved her hand. "This is getting old. We'd better head for class. Let me grab my gear bag and I'll meet you at the front door."

The two walked in a comfortable silence for a while, enjoying the sun, a rare sight in coastal Northern California, where overcast was the norm. A soft gust tousled Gina's short hair. She tucked the amber strands behind her ears and pushed her glasses up.

"Kate?"

"Hmmm?"

"I'm sorry. I shouldn't have brought it up."

"It's okay. Just don't bring it up any more."

"Okay." She paused. "What is it about your sword class that you like so much?"

"I dunno, exactly. There are lots of reasons. It's empowering, for one. And challenging. I can transfer my skills from that *other* sport, so all's not wasted."

"You could say the same for your jujitsu classes."

"True. Look how fast I've gotten my rank advancements. All those years studying routines made it easy for me to remember techniques and combine them in different ways." She paused, choosing her words. "But sword is different. It's mental... like chess. I know people say the same about other martial arts, but—" She hesitated.

3

"Oh, maybe it's just the idea of commanding a weapon. It's so different from anything I've ever done. And swords are just so cool!"

Gina glanced at her, then up at the sky. "You still don't like to talk about it, do you?"

Kate waggled her finger at Gina. "You're bringing it up again." She sighed. "Look, I've tried to explain to people how I feel. Nobody understands why I feel so betrayed. Maybe that's the wrong word." She looked sideways at Gina. "Even you don't understand, Gina. No, don't deny it."

Gina smiled sadly at her friend. "But I'm *trying* to understand. It just seems like such a waste. You were so good and you still are! You could go far."

"But not far enough, Gina. That's the point. Look, I really don't want to talk about it ever again. I just want to forget about it all." Kate looked down at her training sword strapped to her gear bag. "Sword helps me, you know. When you're sparring with people, or receiving others' attacks, you have to be so *there,* so in the moment, that nothing else has any importance. It's one of the things I loved the most about gymnastics. I'm glad I didn't have to give that part up, too."

They were nearing the high school theater. "So, do you want to come to my class this afternoon? You can just sit in on it," Kate asked as they approached the door. "There are only four teachers in the whole United States who instruct in Kashima Shin Ryu, and we've got one of 'em right here in Eureka! You'd be foolish not to take this opportunity to learn from a master instructor. And he's such a great teacher. You'd like him."

Gina rolled her eyes. "I know, I know. It's not like this is the first time in the past three years that you've bugged me about this, you know!" She paused, her hand on the door handle, and looked hard at Kate. "This is really important to you, isn't it?"

Kate was thoughtful. "Yeah, I guess it is. You know how much we liked working out together when we were in gymnastics. I thought if you got into sword as much as I am, then it'd be like old times. I miss that. We hardly see each other anymore."

Gina looked at her friend and smiled. "Well, I can't promise anything. But I can watch one class. I have to admit, I am curious."

"And afterwards, do you want to come with me to the Sullivans' while I sit with Joey? They won't mind."

"If I do, I can't stay too long. I'm meeting Ben at eight. We're working on the *Macbeth* scene together."

"Ahhhhhh, Gentle Ben." Kate winked. "I bet that's not all you'll be working on!"

Gina blushed and punched her in the arm. "Cut it out, Kate."

* * *

Kate bowed off the mat and crossed over to the bench where Gina was sitting, her eyes sparkling.

"You looked good out there," Gina said.

"Yeah? Thanks! I had fun. Come on. If we hurry we can stop off at the Tokyo Express before I have to be at the Sullivans'. I'll buy you a California Roll."

Kate gathered up her gear and the two left the dojo.

"So, Gina, what'd you think of the class?"

"Really interesting. What was that really long weapon you were swinging that curved at the end?"

"A *naginata*. If it had been real, that curved end would have been a really sharp blade. The foot soldiers used them in battle against the infantry to cut the horses' legs off, among other things. Isn't that *sick*?"

"Yeah, pretty gross." An impish smile crossed Gina's face. "Hey, you didn't tell me that Trevor was taking that class."

Kate shrugged. "You never asked."

"You should see the way he looks at you. It's obvious he still cares."

"We're friends, that's all."

"But he is so perfect for you," Gina responded. She began to number off her reasons with her fingers. "For one, he's into what you're into. Second, he's nice, kind, respectful, funny. And three, he's such a *hottie*. "

Kate gave her a sidelong glance. "Sounds to me like Ben's got a little competition."

Gina laughed. "Kate!" She ran her hand through her hair. "Seriously, I never bothered to ask you why you two stopped seeing each other."

"That's because you and I never hang together anymore. If I weren't such a magnanimous friend, I'd be jealous of Benny-boy."

Gina looked contrite. "I'm sorry, Kate. I hate it when girls ditch their friends just because they've got a guy. Now, I realize that I'm one of them! Arrrrghhhh! Shoot me, will you? Just shoot me!"

"Nope, too loud and messy. I'll use a sword."

Having reached her truck, Kate tossed her gear bag into the bed and unlocked the passenger side for Gina. "Sushi still okay?" she asked as she went around to the driver's side and climbed in.

Gina nodded. "It's okay with me. Hey, Kate, why don't you just move to Japan?" she teased.

Kate laughed. "Actually, I may go there this September instead of starting college."

"Really? When did you decide that?"

"Today, during my private lesson with Sensei. He was telling me about some people he knows in Japan I could stay with. It'd be a great opportunity to train at the Kashima Shin Ryu dojo, visit the shrine, get to know Japan. Do some traveling," she said dreamily. "I'll have to see what Mom and Dad think about it." She adjusted her seat belt, pulling her braid out of the way. "Maybe if I went with a friend," she mused. She started the engine, drove the truck out of the parking lot and into the street.

Gina was silent. Kate looked at her. "What?"

"Oh, I was just thinking about graduation. Next fall is going to be so different, with everyone going off their separate ways. It's *big*."

"Yeah, it is big. But I'm so ready, Gina! I want my life to begin! I want an adventure!"

"I just want Ben," Gina replied.

"Girl, you've got Ben. Now, let's get some food!"

* * *

"It's seven forty-five, Kate." Gina got up from the floor. "I need to get going."

Kate looked up at her friend from where she sat with Joey on her lap. The floor was littered with toys. "Wait,'" she said, rising. "I'll go with you to the door." She looked around. "Man, we've really trashed this place!"

Gina took her jacket off the coat rack. "Neat trick, that diaper bag right there," she said. "I'm going to have to remember that."

She glanced around as she zipped up her jacket. "Say, what's that little door under the stairs there? Storage closet?"

Kate followed Gina's gaze. "That's what I thought until I opened it once. It leads into the Sullivans' basement."

"Basement? You don't see many of those around here."

"Well, it's more like a dirt pit. The only things down there are the water heater and furnace. It's kinda gross." Kate crossed over to the small door. "Wanna look?" she asked, hand on the latch.

"No thanks! I'm not *that* curious."

Kate laughed and then her brow furrowed. "Shhhh. I think I hear something!" She opened the door and peered in. "Helloooooo? Anybody down there? *Nobody but us vampires*!" she answered herself.

Gina laughed. "You had me going there…for, like, a whole second."

Kate grinned. "I really did think I heard something, but this house is always making creaking and groaning sounds. You should hear the tree outside Joey's bedroom window when the wind blows." Kate put a fist over her heart. "Babysitting is not for the faint of heart. We babysitters are a brave lot!"

Gina giggled and turned towards the front door.

"This was really fun, Kate. I'm glad I came along. We'll have to do it again, soon, okay?"

Kate smiled. "I'm here every Wednesday. Just let me know when."

"Okay!" Gina held her fingers up for Joey to grasp. "And good night to you, Joey. You are such a cutie." She turned towards the door.

"Don't forget to think about taking sword."

Gina looked serious. "I won't, Kate, but I'm not sure if it's really my thing. Don't get your hopes up, 'k?"

Kate smiled. "It's not for everybody. I was hoping you'd be excited about it but," she shrugged. "Oh, well. Say 'hi' to Ben." And she waved her friend off.

"Well, Joey," Kate began as she walked back into the Sullivans' living room, "it's just you and me and bedtime." She threw him in the air while he let out peals of laughter. "Chubby Boy!" she laughed, and tossed him up again. He squealed his delight, fat little fists clenching and unclenching. "Fly Angel-Boy! Fly!" And she threw him up again. This time she hugged him and planted a big kiss on his soft, fat cheek.

Kate nestled Joey onto her hip and picked up the scattered toys.

"Okay, we're all done here. Let's turn out some lights, and we'll go up to your room."

"How can you be real, Joey?" she asked, as they were climbing the stairs. "You're too perfect. Just look at you!" She tickled him, enjoying his laughter.

Kate flicked on the bedroom lights. She crossed over to the changing table and lay Joey down, turning on the mobile of little animals. Joey's legs kicked with enthusiasm as he watched the dangling animals circle about his head. Kate reached for a clean Pampers and began to change his diaper, chatting to him as she worked.

"I don't know what it is about you, Sweet Boy, but I just love you so!" Kate gazed down at him, smiling at the way he tried to touch the animals circling over his head. "I don't really like babies, you know," she said. "You're the exception."

She put him into his fleece pajamas, tickling him again. He gurgled. "I know! You're a magic baby. You must be! And you've enchanted me to do your bidding."

Kate scooped up his compact little body and carried him back downstairs into the kitchen. "Time for bottle and beddy-bye, my little master." Humming softly, Kate opened the refrigerator, took out a bottle of pre-made formula, and heated it in the microwave. "How's that for instant gratification?" she asked as she tested it on her wrist and then put the bottle into Joey's outstretched little hands.

Sucking from the bottle, Joey sighed and nestled into Kate's arms as she carried him back upstairs to his bedroom.

It was a small room with a crib in one corner, a changing table and a rocking chair nearby. The walls were dark blue with white trim. The glow-in-the-dark stars on the ceiling were in the shapes of the Big and Little Dippers. A recessed window looked out onto a huge, gnarled oak tree, an unusual sight on the Northern Californian coast, where redwoods prevailed.

But there were plenty of redwoods in the front of the Sullivans' Victorian home. The oak had been planted long ago to shade a garden in the back. Now its sprawling branches nearly came into the house. On windy nights, when the branches groaned and scratched the sides of the house, Joey's father threatened to cut it down. But he never did.

Kate pointed at the ceiling. "Ursa Major and Minor looking down on you, Joey. And see, Ursa Minor leads you straight to the North Star, so you can never be lost." Joey merely grunted and snuggled against her. Kate smiled as she watched his eyes getting heavy.

She sank into the rocking chair and smoothed Joey's curls off his forehead as she rocked him. "Would you like to hear a story while you finish? It's all about my favorite little boy." Joey's green eyes found her face and he smiled sleepily behind his bottle. It was still three quarters full. "Looks like I'll have to make this a long story. You've still got a lot left there, buddy."

Kate was thoughtful for a moment. "Okay, Magic Boy...here's my story for tonight." She smiled as she watched his eyes droop and shook him gently. "Hey, wake up! You've a bottle and a story and a nice burping when you're done. What could be better?

"Tonight you're going to learn all about my favorite baby, who's named Joey. He's not an ordinary baby, you see. Well, he's got all his toes and fingers and everything, but he's special. And he looks an awful lot like you."

The oak by the window creaked, and Kate glanced up. "Looks like that tree's giving us some mood music, boyo."

"Now, this special Joey really isn't human. Oh, no, he's something much better. He's a prince from another world, and he's destined for greatness. But those destined for greatness always have enemies, don't you know. So, this Joey, who looks an awful lot like you, has great enemies. These enemies don't want Joey to grow up. These enemies want to hurt Joey. Yes, they want bad things to happen to him."

She looked down at her favorite little guy, peacefully sucking on his bottle, and smiled. "I can see that you're concerned for this Prince Joey. But don't worry, because princes who are destined for greatness also have friends who will do all they can to help them."

Kate paused, thinking about the books she had read and the movies she had seen. "And they usually have lots of luck. And this Prince Joey is no exception. He's a very lucky little baby."

Kate paused, listening to the tree creak again as she thought about the story she was creating. "Man, it's gotten cold in here. Your Mommy must have left that window open. You know how she is about fresh air." Kate moved to rise, but Joey looked at her, disgruntled. She smiled and instead reached for the blanket hanging over the crib and draped it over her lap. "Now that we're both cozy, shall I continue?"

"So, this lucky Prince Joey's friends decide that they must hide him from his enemies so that he can grow up to be a great king and leader. That was the easy part. The hard part was trying to figure out where to hide a little baby. Prince Joey was a newborn, you see. Newborns are noisy and have many needs. Can you remember how noisy you were? I know ten months is a long time to remember back to, but do try."

Kate smiled. "Anyway, the baby prince's friends thought and thought (and fought, too, if you must know) about where would be a safe place to hide him. Finally they decided that there was no place on their world that was safe for Joey. So, they had to hide him on another world. And, voila! They brought you here.

"How, you might wonder? Why, they switched you with another newborn baby. The other baby, poor thing, was a decoy, and that was too bad. Don't think he was badly treated, though. On the contrary, he was loved and cuddled as much as you are. But decoys are always in lots more danger than those being hidden. That's how it works."

Glancing down at Joey, Kate took the bottle from his sleepy grasp. "Good enough, time for burping." She stood up, patting the sleepy child on his back as she carried him to his crib. After summoning a lusty burp, she gently laid him down and covered him with the blanket she had been using to cover her lap. "And that, my little angel boy, is the to-be-continued-story of Prince Joey, who was taken to another world out of harm's way so he could grow into greatness."

Kate bent over the crib to kiss the sleepy little boy, wondering if she would ever have her own children, and if they'd be as sweet as the one lying before her. The idea of having a baby was too hard for her to imagine. She had too much to do first. Too many adventures. She smiled. Gina on the other hand…

Suddenly, she heard the rustle of fabric and a footstep. Her head shot up. She froze.

"How do you come to know these things?" demanded a voice from the recesses of the window, and a figure emerged from the shadows.

Chapter 2- The Walker

Kate whirled around towards the voice, instinctively placing herself between it and the crib. Squinting, she could barely make out the bulky shape beginning to move toward her into the light. A hooded cloak concealed his features, except for the glint of his eyes.

"How —?" The question remained half-formed as she reacted to the threat.

Scooping up Joey, blanket and all, Kate dashed out of the room and down the hall. Fear sped her along as she skidded towards the stairs, grabbing the banister to keep herself from tripping on the rug.

She did not need to look behind her to know that she was being pursued as she raced down the stairs two at a time. Kate reached the front door and jerked it open, finally daring to look behind her as Joey began to wail.

Her attacker was nearly upon her, and her heart leapt in her chest. Looking wildly about, Kate saw the coat rack by the door. She pulled it down into the attacker's path as she dashed outside, grabbing the diaper bag to use as a weapon. She heard a curse, but the obstacle barely slowed him down as he leaped over it and increased his speed.

Kate almost reached the street when she was overtaken and tackled from behind. She tightened her grip on Joey as she braced for a collision with a giant redwood. But the tree *went soft* and Kate felt herself falling into a place she'd never seen before.

For a moment she lay still on her side, trying to acclimate herself. Joey had rolled out of her grasp, and Kate looked wildly about. She saw him a few feet away from her, crying. His little arms waved, fists clenched, and his expression was angry. Looking behind her, she saw the stranger on his knees nearby. His gaze was fixed upon Joey. Kate threw the diaper bag at him, followed closely by a roundhouse kick, but he easily averted the former, and, blocking the latter, quickly captured her leg and forced her down onto her stomach. He sprang on top of her, locking her leg with his own and pinning her arm in an arm-bar.

He spoke again, that same soft voice with the inflections of an accent she could not place. "If you struggle further, girl, I will break your arm." He applied pressure to prove his point.

"Okay, okaaaaaay!," Kate replied between clenched teeth. The pressure stopped, but he did not let go. Instead, Kate was hauled to her feet. "Let me go!" she cried. "I must see to Joey."

"Stop struggling!"

She gasped as he put more pressure on her arm. "Joey. He's crying. I have to go to him."

Her captor was silent. All was still except for Joey's wails. "Very well. See to the babe," he said softly. "But do not try to run from me. I will have my weapon trained upon you. And," he warned, "it is too dangerous for such as you Between Worlds."

Between Worlds?

She was released. Kate stepped unsteadily towards Joey, rubbing her arm. As she crossed to him, she heard the hiss of a sword being drawn.

Joey lay between the roots of a gnarled tree. Kate squatted down beside the baby and scooped him into her arms. She rewrapped him in his blanket and started whispering to him quietly, hugging him to her. But he continued to wail.

"The babe, is he injured?" The concern in the stranger's voice seemed real.

Kate did not bother to glance up. "No, he's just seriously pissed, not that I blame him. Not that I blame him one bit." Kate could feel her own anger replacing the fear she had felt just moments ago. She pushed the emotion aside and focused on calming Joey.

Finally, with a big sigh, Joey snuggled into Kate's warmth and closed his eyes. Kate felt a small sense of satisfaction. She looked up, taking in her surroundings for the first time, deliberately ignoring the stranger behind her.

They appeared to be in the midst of a forest filled with dark, ancient trees. It looked like early winter, or late fall, because the branches which twisted high over Kate's head were bare. Kate couldn't find the light source. Muted browns and grays colored the place. She noticed a soft mist swirling around her legs. A chill ran up her spine, and she rose to her feet. Her grip tightened around Joey.

No! Stay with the anger. Don't get scared!

Feeling the anger returning, she braced herself and turned to challenge the stranger.

"Where are we?" she asked. "And what is going on here? " She tried to make out his face from within the dark recesses of the hood. "You have a lot of explaining to do. Kidnapping is a crime, in case you didn't know."

The stranger slowly pushed the hood from his face, and Kate's eyes widened.

He was young! He looked only a couple of years older than she. By the way he had spoken and handled himself, she had envisioned someone much older, in his thirties at least.

For a moment Kate forgot about where she was standing and about the danger she and Joey were in. She just stood, speechless, gazing at the stranger, her anger all dried up. Silently, she studied him, taking in his dark, hooded cloak, green tunic, dark leather pants that were tucked into scuffed boots—and the sword.

There was something about him that she did not want to admit because it made it harder for her to regain her anger. It did not help that he looked like a beautiful, dark angel…tall, graceful, and strong with his long, dark, braided hair hanging thick down his back. Nor did it help that his eyes were nearly the same jade green color as Joey's. It was his expression that captured her interest. He looked trustworthy, and that bothered her, because she could not explain why she thought he was.

"How do you come to know these things?" the stranger asked again, gesturing towards the now-quiet Joey. "The babe. How do you know about the babe?" He took a step towards her. The sword glinted in his hands, reminding Kate that he was dangerous.

Kate swallowed. "The babe? What things?"

His look darkened and he went very still. "Yes," he said slowly. "Tell me what you know about the Prince, and how you know." He took another step towards her. The sword's metal gleamed as if shining with an inner light.

Kate swallowed again, tasting fear. She backed away from the stranger. He was so still, like a waiting tiger. Kate cleared her throat, shaking her head. "I don't know what you mean," she replied carefully. "This is Joey. I'm his babysitter. I don't know what you're talking about."

"You called him 'Prince' earlier. You knew he was a changeling." His sword tip moved slightly.

Kate's eyes widened. She understood swords. "No! No wait! You don't understand. Please! Put that..." she pointed at the sword, "away. I made the whole story up. Please believe me! It's the truth! I have a very active imagination. I'm always making up stories. You can ask anybody who knows me! It was just a fantasy, a bedtime story."

"A fantasy," he repeated.

"Yes," she replied rapidly. "I mean, stuff like that doesn't exist. It's silly to think otherwise." Kate's mind whirled with confusion. "I mean, that's what I've always thought. But, then," she gestured with her free arm, "this tree thing, and this place? I don't know. I just don't know..." Her voice trailed away under the stranger's steady gaze.

She swallowed.

There were several moments of silence. Kate held Joey more closely as she waited. Then the stranger shrugged and the sword slid smoothly back into its scabbard. "I am not a killer. You will live for now."

Kate slowly let out her breath, unaware that she had even been holding it. She watched him pick up the diaper bag and sling it over his shoulder. The sight would have made her grin if she could only relax. "So, will you take us back now?"

The stranger snorted. "So that the babe can be murdered? I think not, girl."

"Murdered! What are you talking about?"

The stranger studied her again. He replied thoughtfully, "The babe's life is endangered. I will take him. But I cannot take you with us." He was about to say more but something distracted him.

Kate stiffened. "Wait a minute! If you think you can take this baby away with you, then you've got another think coming. Joey belongs back with his family. This is just wrong! In fact, I—"

"Quiet, girl! Be still!" And the sword was again naked in his hand. She had not even seen him draw it.

But this time the sword was directed at something else, something behind her. The stranger crouched, holding his sword with two hands, low, in the same manner she had been taught. He gestured with his head, indicating that she and Joey should move behind him.

He didn't have to tell her twice. The very atmosphere seemed to be changing. The mist was thickening and, looking from behind the cloaked figure of the stranger, Kate thought she saw one or two shapes coming into view, very large shapes with eyes that glowed a strange bluish-purple.

"It is not good to linger long in the Place-Between-Worlds." The stranger glanced quickly at Kate, holding his hand out to her. "Take my hand, girl. We go."

She looked at the outstretched hand and hesitated. She squinted at the shapes. What were they? "Now!" the stranger ordered.

Kate stood, immobilized by indecision. After all, moments earlier he had threatened to kill her.

Then she heard a low growl that vibrated in her chest, answered by another. The creatures' eyes seemed to glow brighter. Kate grasped the stranger's outstretched hand.

Before she had time to react, the stranger had pulled her into the closest tree. She tightened her grip on Joey, closed her eyes, and followed. She felt as if she were going through plastic that stretched and then gave way. And then she was somewhere else.

She heard traffic and water sprayed her face. "What the—?"

Kate opened her eyes. They were standing next to a huge fountain made up of boulders cemented together to form a seven-foot waterfall. "Hey! I know where we are! We're—" Kate stopped as Joey, wakened by the fountain's water, let out a happy squeal. She looked down to smile at him, but Joey wasn't looking at her. He was looking at the stranger with his hands outstretched, as if wanting to be picked up. *Joey knew the stranger!*

The stranger smiled at the baby. "Ioho," he said.

Kate drew a breath. "How?" she paused and swallowed, her throat feeling thick and tight. "I mean, what's happening here?" She couldn't keep her voice from rising sharply. It seemed thin and reedy to her ears. Not like her voice at all.

The stranger looked at her questioningly. She tried to focus on him, but he seemed to be close and then far away, and she couldn't tell exactly where he was standing. Her ears were ringing, and she couldn't seem to catch her breath. Kate reached out blindly with her free hand, trying to find something to hold onto.

"Breathe." She heard his voice above the ringing in her ears. She felt a strong arm about her shoulders, keeping her on her feet. She took a deep breath and let it out. She took another. "Sit," the voice said, and she did, her head slowly clearing.

Kate looked at Joey in her lap laughing up at her. She stroked his soft hair. At that moment she needed him more than he had ever needed her. He was her anchor in a world that had suddenly—too suddenly—gone strange.

"Better?"

Kate glanced up at the stranger. He did not look quite as threatening as he had before. She nodded.

"Please," Kate said weakly. "I really need to know what is going on here."

The stranger leaned down and touched her shoulder. "Yes," he agreed. "It is only fair that you be told."

He looked around, scanning the area.

18

"I shall reserve a room in that inn." He pointed toward the Best Western Hotel. "You will come with me. You will not run or bring attention to yourself or the babe. If you should do so, I will stop you. This babe is in grave danger, and you are ill prepared to protect him. There are some who will stop at nothing to see him dead. Do you understand me?"

Kate could read the stranger's determination in his expression as he waited for her answer. She glanced around, taking in her surroundings. She knew exactly where she was. She was sitting on a curb by the fountain that was located between a Marie Callender's Restaurant and a Best Western Hotel in Eureka, California. To her right was the mall with the new bookstore where, not two days ago, she had spent more than thirty dollars on Japanese anime books. How could things change so quickly, she wondered?

She sighed. "Yes, I understand. I won't run," she said, looking at the stranger. *Not yet, anyway,* she silently added to herself.

"Good."

Kate watched the stranger warily as he checked them into a room. It wasn't until they were safely in that room that she realized what had been troubling her throughout the whole transaction. "How come that desk clerk didn't freak out talking to a guy dressed like Robin Hood who happened to be carrying a samurai sword?" she asked.

Chapter 3 – The Prophecy

The stranger shrugged. "Because that is not what he saw."

"Oh?"

He hesitated. "It is something I can do. I will explain it to you after I gather some information from your television. I need to see if I am able to anticipate what the assassin will do next."

"*Assassin*? What assassin?"

"The one sent to kill the babe." The stranger looked at Kate more closely. "Are you feeling well?"

Kate took a deep breath. "Yeah, I think so. My ears started to ring again." She shook her head, trying to regain her focus. She gave a little laugh. "I'm going to take care of Joey," she announced. "Maybe if I concentrate on normal things, I can deal with the abnormal ones."

The stranger quietly studied her as she made a little pillow nest for Joey. "I am called Ash. And you?"

She glanced up, shaking her bangs from her eyes. "Kate. Kate Johnson."

"Kate. That is a good name. And the babe is called Joey?"

She nodded. "He recognized you."

"That is the truth. He does know me," Ash answered.

"How? How can Joey know you?"

Ash held his hand up. "A moment, Kate. I need information."

He turned on the television and began to switch channels while Kate made Joey comfortable. He paused at a broadcast giving live coverage of a house fire.

Kate glanced up and stiffened. *"Oh my God! That's the Sullivans' home! What happened?"* She fell silent at Ash's stern look, and together they watched the newscaster.

"…No one is quite sure what started the fire," the newscaster was saying. "Neighbors report hearing an explosion."

"So, it is Straif," Ash commented.

The camera panned back revealing a couple holding a crying baby.

"That's Joey!" Kate looked wildly at the sleeping baby on the bed. "But, I don't understand."

Ash touched her shoulder. "I will explain, Kate."

But Kate wasn't listening to him. She continued to watch the television. "…babysitter who is believed to still be in the building behind me." Kate gasped. "Names are being withheld until the parents are contacted."

Kate headed to the phone, but Ash reached it first. "No, Kate."

"But my parents! They have to know I'm all right!"

"Not yet. Ioho's life is still in danger," Ash stated calmly.

She gestured to the television. "But how could anyone be alive in that? Please, I need to call them. They'll be hysterical!"

"Not yet," he repeated. "They have sent Straif to kill the babe. I should have guessed. He is the Head Assassin for the House of Lophft. The danger that we are in is very great. We cannot act until I have a plan."

"But—"

"If I allowed you to call your parents, then not only would Straif find you, he would find your parents as well. You do not understand about Straif. He is a killer. He has a target—the babe—and he will stop at nothing to carry out his assignment. That means that he will hunt down any person linked to Ioho and extract information any way that he can." Ash paused. "It is not a pleasant notion."

Kate backed away from the phone and switched off the television. "Then," she said, folding her arms, "you had better tell me what is going on before I totally lose my mind."

Ash nodded, unfastening his cloak and laying it on the bed.

"You are strong, Kate," he said while drawing up a chair. "You will adjust to your circumstances. This I do know." He sat, facing the door with his sword in his lap.

"Sit."

Kate sat on the bed close to Joey.

Ash took a breath. "I am Ash of the House of Brendt from the land of Ruis." He nodded at Joey who had fallen back to sleep. "And that babe is Ioho, my young cousin." He glanced at Kate. "I will attempt to be brief."

"Nearly two hundred years ago there was an uprising and, through deception and betrayal, the throne was taken away from the House of Brendt by the House of Lophft. Those were dangerous times. Many innocents were slaughtered, and our only option was to go into hiding; our only hope was the Prophecy."

"Prophecy?" Despite her fear and confusion, Kate's curiosity was aroused.

"Yes. In our holy book, the Book of Phagos, it speaks of a prince who, upon reaching manhood, will bring together the exiled people and end the tyranny."

"And you think Joey is the prince?" she asked softly.

"I know it to be the truth. Ioho is the prince we have been waiting for."

"Whoa." She glanced at Joey and back at Ash. "I swear I was only making that story up. I had no idea it could be true."

Ash looked at her seriously. "I am not a Truth Knower, Kate, so I must trust your word on that. But I do know you would not hurt Ioho."

"No way would I ever hurt him!"

"This is good. I have sworn to give my life in defense of my young cousin."

The look in his eyes gave Kate little doubt that he meant what he said, and she heard the threat in his voice.

"I will not hurt Joey," she repeated. "So," Kate went on when Ash didn't respond. "How do you know that Joey is the prince that you have been waiting for?"

"There have been signs, predictions that have come true. Especially about the birth—the day, the hour. The parents. All the signs were there."

Kate squinted at him. "You looked funny just then, when you mentioned Joey's parents."

Ash sighed. "The mother, she was from the House of Brendt. The father was from the House of Lophft."

"Was?"

"Aye. The babe's father was killed when we discovered his lineage. He was a prince, you understand. He was dangerous. He had learned too many of our secrets."

Ash rubbed his face with one hand.

"Ioho's mother never forgave us. She lost the will to live and died during childbirth."

"Oh, that's sad," Kate said softly.

"Aye. These are sad times. But there is hope. As long as Ioho lives, hope lives."

"Is that why you brought Joey—Ioho—here? To keep him safe, like I said in my story?"

"That is true." Ash studied the sleeping infant. "I wonder…"

"What?"

"On Ruis, we are each of us born with a gift. It is said that Ioho will have many gifts. I am simply wondering if perhaps you did not conceive of the bedtime story on your own. Perhaps…"

"Perhaps what?" Kate grinned. "Are you telling me that Joey mentally put the story in my head?"

"Exactly so."

Kate laughed. "That's not possible! For one thing, Joey's a ten-month-old baby, for crying out loud! For another, how can people put their thoughts into another's mind? Not possible."

But Ash simply shook his head. "You asked me earlier how it was I can move freely in your world without others noticing my dress."

"I did." Kate was still smiling.

"Look again, Kate."

Her smile faded. Before her sat an Ash dressed in a white button-down shirt, wool blazer jacket and jeans. Instead of boots, he wore loafers. The sword on his lap was a cane. Even his hair was short, the thick braid gone. He looked well groomed and respectable.

Kate simply stared at him, her mouth opening and closing, eyes wide, the bedspread clenched in her fists.

Ash grinned and returned to his original dress. "You look like a fish, Kate."

"Not funny, Ash! That wasn't possible. How can you make me see those things? I don't like this." Her voice started to rise.

Ash's smile vanished. He reached out a hand as if to touch her. "I apologize, Kate. I did not mean to frighten you. These things…this night…it must be very strange to you."

"Strange is not the half of it. I really don't know what to think, here." But her grip on the bedspread had loosened.

"You are very brave, Kate."

Kate snorted. "Brave? To tell you the truth, I am barely holding it together. I just keep looking at Joey and thinking about the practical things. If I didn't, I think I'd totally lose it. No, I'm not brave."

"I disagree, Kate. I have witnessed others in similar situations and you *are* brave." Ash smiled at her and Kate felt ridiculously pleased with herself.

"So what's going on, Ash?"

"I do not understand the question."

"Why are you sure Joey is going to be killed?"

"Ah, I see. It is complicated. Simply put, there is a traitor among the Brendt. Before Ioho was born, the Council decided that I should bring him here for safety. Thus, at Ioho's birth, I switched him with the Sullivan child. Ioho was to be raised as their son while I kept watch over him. As he grew, I would instruct him in our ways. When it was time, I would bring him back to Ruis so he might fulfill the Prophecy.

"However, the traitor told Lophft where Ioho was being hidden. I was immediately told to fetch Ioho, bring him back to Ruis, and replace him with the Sullivans' true son. But plans change, do they not?" he asked wryly. "I heard you speaking to Ioho, and I had to know how much you knew. These are dangerous times, and we must overlook nothing. You may be a threat."

"I'm no threat!"

"Aye, I hope that to be true, for I have already told you more than common sense would allow."

"So, what happens next?"

"I must assume that Ioho's life continues to be threatened. I am in hope that Straif will be focused on killing the Sullivan babe and..."

"Oh no! That's horrible.

"These are dangerous times, Kate."

"But that little *baby!*"

"Straif will not kill that babe unless he finds the mark. When he does not find the mark, he will begin to hunt anew."

"The mark?"

"Yes, like this one." And Ash pushed up his sleeve revealing the profile of a bear tattooed onto a well-muscled forearm. "This is the Great Bear of the House of Brent. All whose blood is of the House of Brendt have this sign tattooed onto their skin at birth."

"But Joey doesn't have a bear on his arm. Oh—," Kate looked at the baby. "His birthmark. It's not a birthmark is it? It's been...changed, hasn't it? Like how you made me see you in different clothes."

25

"You are clever, Kate," Ash answered.

"So this Straif person won't kill that other baby unless he finds that tattoo?"

"It is what we can hope. Fortunately, we are not on Ruis. Straif needs to be subtle."

Ash stretched. "There are a few hours, and I shall rest. Then, before dawn, I will take Ioho to Ruis."

"How do you get there? To Ruis?"

"I will take him there."

"But how?"

"What is the method?"

Kate nodded.

"I am a Walker-Between-Worlds. That is my gift. I can find the portals between the worlds, and I simply go there.

Kate was thoughtful. "At the Sullivans'…that tree. Was that tree a portal?"

"Most trees can be used as portals, yes."

"So when I hit the tree, that place we went to? Was that Ruis?" Kate gave a shudder.

"No. That is the Place-Between-Worlds. It is simple to explain. When I Walk, I go from one place—such as Ruis—to the Place-Between-Worlds, and then to another place, such as Earth."

"Are there many worlds, then?"

"Yes, many. So many that we Walkers have barely begun to explore them."

"Don't you ever get lost?"

"No. Never. It is my gift."

"But others?"

"Suffice it to say that you would never want to travel between worlds without a Walker. And you never, ever want to linger in the Place-Between-Worlds. There is much evil there. Dark things."

Kate shuddered, remembering the purple eyes that glowed. "This is all so unbelievable."

"I assure you, Kate, that it is all true."

"I know that. It's just so hard to think right now."

Ash stood up and checked the door. "It is time to rest. We only have a few hours." He glanced at Kate warily.

"What? You don't think I'm going to run away, do you?"

"I saw your concern for your parents, Kate. I can take no chances."

"I won't run, ok? You have my word."

Ash smiled gently. "I know you will not run. Sit back down, Kate." And he pulled a cord from a pocket within the folds of his cloak.

Kate held her hands up and backed away from him. "Oh no. No, that is not going to happen." Ash lifted an eyebrow. "You are not going to tie me up. No way, Ash."

Chapter 4 - Ruis

An hour later, Kate was still awake. She glanced at the cord tied to her ankle and followed it to where it was tied to Ash's ankle. *At least he let me go to the bathroom,* she thought, and sighed and re-crossed her ankles. She looked at his dark outline, studying him as she formulated her question.

"Are you awake?" Kate could see a glint from his eyes, giving her the answer.

"What is it that you need, Kate?"

They were sitting, facing each other, legs propped up on the hotel coffee table that they had pulled between them.

"Let me go with you, to Ruis. I don't want to say good-bye to Joey in this room. I want to make sure that he'll be safe."

She was answered by silence.

"Ash?"

She heard him shift. "It is not wise. It is dangerous."

"It's all dangerous. Please?" Kate waited. "Look, I need to see where he's going to be living."

"It's not done. Walkers do not bring others to Ruis."

"But it's not like I'm going to live there! I'll only be there for, what, ten minutes? Only enough time for me to see Joey safely in his new life. How can that hurt anything?"

More silence.

"Please understand! I love Joey, and after tonight I'm never going to see him again!"

"It's best that you do not know too much. For your safety."

"But I already know too much, don't I? What can it hurt for me to know just a little more? It's not like I'd ever be able to follow you back again. *You're* the Walker, not me."

"You are persistent, are you not?"

"So I have been told."

Ash sighed. "Very well. It will happen as you wish."

"Thanks. I really thank you… It means a lot to me."

"Now rest." And he settled deeper into his chair.

Kate tried to rest, but so much had happened in such a short time. Thoughts raced across her mind. She glanced at Ash's dark form across from her. He was like no one she had ever met before. He reminded her of one of the heroes from Japanese anime, beautiful, strong, dangerous, yet filled with honor. Only better. She smiled. Ash was real.

And Ruis. She was actually going to Ruis! Kate felt her stomach leap with excitement. What would it be like? And when she got back? Would anyone believe her? Probably not. And so she would have to keep it all a secret. That was going to be so hard! Maybe she could write a story about it all, maybe sell it and make tons of money. Then she could travel and buy her parents a huge home. *Her parents!*

Kate jerked up, accidentally pulling on the cord.

Instantly Ash was on his feet, sword at the ready.

"Oh my God!" Kate gasped. "I didn't know anyone could move that fast! I'm so sorry, Ash."

Ash re-sheathed his sword and sat down again. "What is it?" he asked patiently.

"I'm really sorry," she said again. "But I was thinking about things, and all of a sudden I realized that when I get back here from Ruis, I'm going to have to come up with some sort of reason for my not being dead. I mean, everyone thinks I was in that fire."

Ash sighed and reached behind himself to switch on a lamp. "Since neither of us is in the mood to sleep, we might as well think through this riddle while we wait."

* * *

Just before dawn, Ash took one last look around the hotel room before he shut the door. He glanced at Kate, "Ready?"

She nodded and looked down at Joey riding on her hip. He was awake and quietly watchful. *He's going to need to eat soon,* she thought, *and be changed.* She felt a pang of real regret. In such a short time Joey was going to be gone from her forever.

They took the stairs and headed for the back of the hotel.

"Why not use that stone fountain again?" Kate wondered.

"Trees make the best portals," Ash explained. "I discovered that I could use that fountain by accident. As a rule, Walkers use trees. I was curious to see if other objects could be used as portals."

"Why the fountain? It's a pretty public spot."

"The pie."

"What?"

"That restaurant by the fountain has lovely pie. Oftimes I would come from Ruis to eat the pie."

Kate laughed.

They stopped in front of a large shrub, its twisted branches dry and brittle.

"Are you prepared, Kate?"

She looked skeptically at the bush. "That's your portal? What about a tree?"

"Kate, it is time. Come. Take my hand."

Kate clasped Ash's hand and closed her eyes. As she stepped forward, she once more felt the sensation of pushing through plastic and then, in another step, it was over. Opening her eyes, Kate found that she was in the Place-Between-Worlds. Her hand tightened on Ash's, and she drew Joey closer to her, amazed at his alert silence.

Ash led them towards a nearby tree. It was ancient, thick and bent with age. This time, Kate kept her eyes open as they stepped through. Her senses reeled as her eyes were dazzled with a momentary fire-burst of color. She nearly walked into Ash. "Oh, I think I did better keeping my eyes closed," she gasped. "That was way too trippy!"

"Hush," Ash whispered, and motioned for her to follow him.

They stood on the edge of a large clearing in the midst of a vast forest, the early morning light casting long shadows. The sun glinted off dew-laden spider webs. The breeze was soft and balmy.

In the middle of the clearing was a circle of wagons. In the middle of the wagons was another circle of square-topped tents, all facing onto a common area where Kate could see several fire pits encircled by stones. The flooring of the common area looked to be some type of woven matting. There was a much larger tent on one side of the circle. The design of the encampment seemed to Kate to be quite practical. "It looks like a wagon train from old Westerns I've seen on TV," she murmured to herself.

It did not take her long to realize that the three of them seemed to be the only people in the area.

"Wait here," Ash whispered and, before Kate could nod, he had disappeared into the forest like a shadow. She tried to follow him with her eyes, but quickly lost track. He moved so quietly, and his dark cloak blended into the shadows.

In a few moments, Kate caught a glimpse of Ash cautiously entering the encampment from the opposite side of the clearing. He disappeared into a tent, only to reappear. Methodically he checked each tent in the circle and finally, the largest tent at the end.

Kate waited for him, taking in her surroundings and listening to the forest sounds, feeling as if she were back on Earth. Joey sighed, and she looked at him. He had been so quiet. "Are you hanging in there, buddy?" Kate asked. His eyes fastened on her, and he gave a little burble of contentment. "You'll be having breakfast, soon. You'll see, my little prince-boy."

"Come, Kate!" Ash called. He was holding something.

As she neared, he held up what looked like a canvas chair in a wooden harness. "I believe this can make your burden more comfortable for you." Ash explained. "I found it in one of the tents."

"Oh! A baby-backpack! Nice!" She quickly handed Joey over to Ash as she put the backpack on and strapped it about her waist, pulling her braid out of the way. "This will make things much easier. Thanks, Ash. That was really thoughtful."

Ash smiled and put Joey in the pack, where he delightedly patted Kate's head as Ash strapped him in.

"Easy on the horsey, prince-boy." Kate said, laughing. Then she sobered. "So, Ash, where is everybody?"

"I do not know, Kate. This is troubling." He glanced at her. "I think we should be better prepared. Come with me."

Kate followed Ash into the main tent. It appeared to be made out of canvas lashed together with strips of leather. The entry panel was painted with ornate designs and complicated multicolored whorls. Kate paused, "This is beautiful, Ash! It reminds me of the Celtic patterns back home."

"I am not surprised," he answered. "Come."

He led her into the tent and Kate's eyes widened with pleasure.

The inside of the enormous tent was beautiful and sensual. The reed flooring was strewn with thick carpets woven in beautiful patterns. Oil lamps hung from the ceilings. To one side were a large banquet table and benches. On the other, canvas chairs were arranged in clusters for conversation and stuffed with colorful pillows for comfort. In the center was a large fire pit surrounded with stacked stones. There was an opening in the top of the tent to allow smoke to escape. Diaphanous fabrics in multi colors hung from the ceiling, gently swaying in the air. Kate took a step toward the fire pit, marveling at the beauty of the deep burgundy and sapphire rug beneath her feet.

Ash touched her arm. "Kate! There is no time right now. We must find my Kinsmen. Here, pick one of these."

Kate turned, facing the doorway. On either side were rows of weapons, neatly arranged as to their function.

"Are there any that you can use?" Ash asked. "I do not know how much fighting skill you have."

"Not much, Ash. Not much at all. I know some jujitsu and kempo. And I really love my kenjitsu class." Ash looked confused. "Oh, you probably don't know those terms."

She looked at the rows of weapons. "It doesn't matter." She crossed over to a group of weapons of similar shapes but different lengths. They reminded her of the *naginata* that she practiced her swings with. She chose a shorter one and picked it up, feeling its balance, studying the curved tip of the blade. "I've never held one of these with a real blade," she explained. "All the weapons I use are for practice and are wooden. The only things I've ever cut with a live blade were reed mats soaked in water. I'm not sure I'd know what to do with this thing. It might be better if I didn't have it."

"You are on Ruis now, Kate, and you carry Prince Ioho on your back. By all appearances, my Kinsmen have deserted this encampment quite suddenly. It can only mean trouble. I say you should be armed."

He crossed over to the banquet table in the back of the tent. For the first time Kate noticed the food that was laid there, baskets of fruit and bread, platters of cold meats and cheeses. Ash reached for a loaf of bread and tore off a chunk. "Breakfast for the babe."

"I don't know, Ash. Is there anything softer? Oatmeal or something?"

They scanned the table, but could find nothing that resembled baby food. Joey squealed and reached for the bread still in Ash's hands.

Kate shrugged. "Well, maybe he can suck on the bread."

Ash placed the bread in Joey's hands. The baby immediately began to gum it. Ash grinned. "It appears he knows what to do." He put the rest of the loaf into a pouch on the backpack. "We must go now."

They were headed for the entrance when the shrill cry of a bird halted Ash in his tracks. He motioned for Kate to get behind him, and they quietly crossed to the entrance, where he peered out into the dawn.

In the sudden stillness they could hear the heavy tread of soldiers and shouts of commands being given. Kate touched Ash's arm in fear. "Quietly, come with me," he whispered. His calmness reassured her.

They ran across the thick carpeting to the very back of the tent. Ash drew his blade and sliced a large opening in the canvas. Together, they peered out through the slit.

"Do you see the tree that I used as a portal?" Ash's mouth was close to her ear. She nodded. "I am going to make a diversion. When you hear the shouting, run to that tree. No matter what happens, Kate, you *must* reach that tree. I will come get you. Look at me, Kate." What he saw in her glance made him nod with satisfaction. "I am going now. Get to the tree. Go as quietly as possible." He squeezed her arm. "I am trusting you, Kate. I am trusting you with Ioho."

Kate nodded, her face grim. Ash left and headed back toward the tent's entrance. For a moment, Kate felt the bitter taste of fear. She wanted to call Ash back to them and feel safe.

But it was only for a moment. "Okay, Joey," she whispered. "I can do this. Don't be scared." She touched his small hand, strengthened her grasp on the *naginata*, and crouched, tensed in readiness.

Hearing shouts, she took a deep breath, exhaled slowly, and quietly slipped through the opening Ash had made.

She ran as quickly and as quietly as she could across the open space, heading toward the nearest wagon. She reached the wagon and paused, looking behind her. She saw about thirty foot soldiers dressed in leather and chain mail, and armed with swords, knives, crossbows and spears. As she listened to their shouts, she felt an adrenalin rush coming to the aid of her fear.

"There he goes!" said a voice.

"Where?" asked another.

"There! Heading towards the wood. Shoot him!" A dozen arrows zinged into the woods.

"Fools! Don't kill him! We need to question him!"

"By the Book! It's a Walker! Keep him away from the forest!"

"A Walker! A Walker!" The cry was taken up. "Circle around him! Keep him from the trees!"

Suddenly Joey sneezed, and Kate flattened herself against the wagon. Had anyone heard? She had her own tree to reach. The sneeze galvanized her into action.

She looked at her destination. It was about fifty feet from where she stood. She took a deep breath.

"Keep searching!" a voice commanded. "There could be more!" It sounded close. Too close.

Kate ran, focusing on her target. Halfway there, she tripped on a hidden branch and stumbled, nearly falling, Joey's weight in the backpack unbalancing her.

"Look, there! A woman!"

"Shit!" whispered Kate, and she ran even faster, the tree getting closer with every step.

She was nearly there when three soldiers broke through the wagons and headed directly into her path. She managed to dodge one, nearly dislodging Joey, who had begun to squeal with delight. She held her *naginata* in front of her as she ran toward the other two. They melted out of her way. She was at the tree!

Kate turned, bracing herself against its trunk, and faced her attackers. She waited, *naginata* in *mugamae*, the stance of nothingness.

The three soldiers gathered around the tree. They looked no older than she, but the gleam in their eyes spoke volumes.

"A babe! She has a babe!" one said.

The middle one seemed to be in charge. Without taking his eyes off of her, he shouted to an unknown captain. "We've got her, sir! Trapped by a tree!" Then he spoke to his companions, "Keep your blades at the ready, mates. I want a closer look."

He inched forward, eyeing Kate. Then he glanced at Joey. "Who's this little babe? I'd like to take a closer look at his forearm, that I would."

"No!" Kate replied. "You will not touch him!"

But the leader ignored her and took another step, drawing his sword. One of the leader's companions shouted a warning.

Kate simply reacted. She did not realize that she had even moved until it was over. She stepped forward, and, with all her might, cut a *kesa* as she had done hundreds of times before.

But this time, the diagonal swing did not cut the air in front of her. This time, the blade of her *naginata* connected with leather, mail and, finally, with muscle, tissue and bone as it sank deeply into the leader's chest. From shoulder to chest a thin red line formed. For an instant time stood still while Kate, her hand still gripping the handle of the weapon, watched, transfixed, as more and more blood began to flow from the wound. Then she raised her eyes and met the soldier's gaze.

His eyes were wide, filled with fear and surprise. As his companions stood frozen in place, the leader dropped his sword. Slowly his hands encircled the blade sticking out from his chest, cutting his fingers as he desperately tried to pull it out. More blood began to flow from the wound, his hands and, as he coughed, from his mouth. Kate's stomach lurched.

"Oh, my Goooodddddd! I'm so sorry! Oh, my God! I'm so sorry! So sorry!" She repeated the words over and over like a mantra.

The leader fell to his knees, his companions each gripping an arm as they helped him stay upright. He gasped for air, hands clenching and unclenching in spasms. Then he sagged forward, head lolling. His companions dropped him, and with a shout they rushed at Kate, who watched them approach as if in a dream.

At that instant, Ash's face appeared from the tree she was braced against, followed by his hands. Startled, the soldiers faltered. Ash grabbed Kate by her braid and the backpack and pulled her through the portal he had created. He half-carried, half-dragged her through the second portal as her stomach lurched and she collapsed into dry heaves, tears streaming down her face.

Chapter 5 - Straif

Straif lay on his belly in a small culvert near the house, waiting to see what his handiwork would flush out. His long legs were crossed, his chin resting on his fists. His dark blond hair fanned across his back. Behind him squatted his Walker. Beside him was his rucksack, which was lighter now that he had placed the explosives beneath the house.

Straif enjoyed his off-Ruis assignments. He enjoyed blowing things up. On Ruis explosives were banned, since they were non-Ruis products. However, other assassins were known to use them on occasion. But Straif took personal pride in working within the limitations of the local environment. He strove to make his killings appear as accidental as possible. It was his signature. If one wanted a killing not to look like a killing, one contracted the Head Assassin of the House of Lophft.

Straif was also one of the few assassins to take off-Ruis assignments. He liked the challenge. And the pay.

Straif shifted positions slightly, estimating that the explosion would occur in just a few moments.

Suddenly, a figure burst forth from the house. Straif tensed, alert. It was a woman carrying a child. Close behind her was a man wearing the traditional cloak of a Walker. He, too, was carrying a child, which he carefully placed on the sidewalk just before he and the woman dove through a portal. Straif felt the explosion within the house just before it shattered the lower windows. Then all was briefly still before smoke began trailing out through the building's openings. Dogs began to bark. Porch lights flickered on.

For a brief moment the intensity of his fury immobilized Straif. In one fluid motion he rose and, slinging the rucksack over his left shoulder, he motioned for the Walker to follow. "I've seen enough," he growled. "Take me back."

Without a word, the Walker reached out and grasped Straif by the forearm. The two disappeared into the nearest tree, oblivious to the shouts of neighbors and the wails of the child who was left on the sidewalk.

* * *

Straif's boots echoed off the walls as he strode down the long, shadowed hallway. The ceiling was so high that the torches lining the hall barely reflected off the rafters. "We must report," Straif called over his shoulder.

The Walker had thrown back her hood, and she strove now to keep up with him. They had worked together several times. It was not the first time she had witnessed his failure. Usually he would take it in stride, knowing that he would eventually dispatch his target. This was the first time she had ever seen him so angry.

Straif reached out and, with a jerk, flung open the doors of the Council room, startling the guards.

Within the room, warmed by a blazing fire, Ogdan the Elder, Head Council Member of Lophft, raised his eyes calmly. He was a slight man enveloped in burgundy robes. His hair was sparse and his eyes burned intensely. "Well?" he asked.

Straif slammed a fist down onto the Council table. "Report!" he spat.

AnnWyn, Straif's Walker, stepped forward. She paused for a moment, catching her breath. It was their custom that she would narrate the events while Straif filled in the details. AnnWyn glanced briefly at Straif before beginning.

"We arrived at the scene according to schedule and without incident," she began. "We cloaked ourselves," she continued. "Straif set the explosives under the dwelling. It was to be a fire caused by a faulty heating device which the people of Earth use inside their dwellings." She glanced at Straif, who had begun pacing back and forth. "Shortly before the explosion, there was activity from the dwelling. Two individuals, a woman and then a man, a Walker—"

"It was Ash!" exclaimed Straif. "By the Head of the Anointed One! How did he know?"

Ogdan the Elder calmly held up his hand. He nodded to AnnWyn. "Continue," he said placidly.

AnnWyn glanced again at Straif. "Both the woman and the man were carrying infants. The man laid his down before they threw themselves into their portal. The explosion nearly caught them." She folded her hands and bowed her head.

Straif smacked his fist against his hand. "How could he have known?" he demanded. "It is just not possible!"

Silence filled the room, interrupted by pops and fizzes from the wood in the fireplace.

"My father, Theron!" said Straif suddenly. "Where is he? *Where is my father?*"

"Theron is gone," Ogdan replied.

Straif's eyes widened. "How?"

The Council member shrugged.

Straif swore in fury, clenching his fists. "It explains how Ash knew. Why was he not watched?"

"Of course he was watched. You know his gift as well as I, Straif. A man like that!"

"He should have been dispatched when we had him!" Straif spat.

AnnWyn gasped.

"Calm yourself, Straif, and think," the Council Head stated irritably. "Theron is of royal blood and an ambassador. We must work within protocol. The Ambassador has fled. If he abides by the regulations, he will be back by tomorrow evening. If he does not, then we will act as protocol dictates."

"And my assignment? What of that?"

"It cannot be helped. We are taking alternative measures."

"What kind of measures?"

"As you recall, your father also told us the location of the main encampment of the House of Brendt. That is where Ash will take the child. We will capture him there with the babe."

Straif began to pace once more. "It is not so easy to capture a Walker," he said, "especially Ash. I know him well."

"A squadron of our best has been dispatched," Ogdan replied. "We will get him."

"Alive?"

"Of course, alive! Now, calm yourself, Straif. Your emotions are overwhelming your judgment."

But Straif was not listening.

"No! I cannot trust that. The woman…" He said as he paced back and forth, his cloak swirling about at each turn. "I must return to Earth. I do not think I have finished with that place just yet." He paused.

"Perhaps you feel we were not thorough enough with our questioning of Theron," suggested Ogden.

"No," Straif replied. "This is a mystery that my father did not know. What are the Brendt plotting? I must return and uncover the identity of that woman!"

"You forget your assignment, Straif," the Council member replied.

Straif stopped pacing and looked at Ogdan the Elder. "That I have not," he answered. "However, as you told me yourself, you have taken measures. My specialties are no longer needed."

"What are you suggesting, Straif?"

"AnnWyn, what did you see just prior to the explosion?" Straif asked the Walker.

She again stepped forward. "I saw a woman and a man emerge from the dwelling. Each was carrying an infant. The man set his infant down, and they then dove through a portal."

Straif touched AnnWyn lightly on the shoulder, and she stepped back from the table. He looked at the Council member. "May I repeat, sir, 'a woman and a man.' Does this not bother you?"

Ogdan leaned forward and placed his elbows upon the table, his fingertips touching, forming a steeple. "Of course it does. Very much so," he replied.

"Then command me to return to Earth. Allow me to investigate and flush out the others. I will eliminate this threat to the House of Lophft."

"We do not know if there is an actual threat, Straif. And it is not my place to reassign you to a different target."

"But it *is* your place, sir, if you deem it necessary."

The Council member glanced at AnnWyn. The Walker's eyes were lit with curiosity. "You are forgetting, Straif, that we are not alone." His eyes hardened and AnnWyn paled.

Straif put a hand on her shoulder. "AnnWyn is loyal to Lophft. We have worked together on several missions now." AnnWyn smiled gratefully up at Straif. His grip tightened on her shoulder. "And," he continued, "she knows who I am and what I do. She also knows what I *would* do if she were disloyal in any way."

The Walker stiffened and tried to break free of Straif's grasp. "But you would not! You could not!" she cried. "It is death to the one who maims or kills a Walker!" she exclaimed, her eyes wide.

Straif looked down at her, one eyebrow cocked. "Did I mention maiming or killing you, AnnWyn?" He laughed softly. "There are other ways to cause pain." As he spoke, his face blended and faded and reshaped itself into the face of a young girl.

AnnWyn gasped. "I-I-sabelle. You would hurt my darling girl? After all that we have been to each other?" Her eyes glistened with unshed tears.

Straif laughed as his face slid back to its normal shape. "Of course I will not hurt Isabelle. She is such a delightful little thing." He looked at AnnWyn hard. "I do not believe it would come to that, do you?" he asked slowly.

"Very touching," Ogdan stated. "And too dramatic for my tastes, Straif. But then I've never met a shapeshifter who could resist showing off. It must be part of their makeup." The chair made a rasping sound as the Council member rose to his feet. "There are only a few hours before dawn. I suggest the two of you rest, as I will need you to report your findings to the Council." He paused. "Shall we continue at nine bells?"

* * *

Straif and AnnWyn did not speak as they followed the maid down the long corridor, across the main receiving room—a cavernous room draped extravagantly with gilded tapestries and candle chandeliers—and into the guest quarters where rooms had been prepared for them.

But, as the door closed behind the maid, AnnWyn turned to Straif, her eyes once more filled with tears. "That was very cruel, what you did back there."

Straif paused while unbuttoning his tunic and looked at AnnWyn as she stood, one hand on the door. Their eyes locked. "Aye, it was cruel," he acknowledged quietly. "But I meant it, nonetheless." He turned from her and continued to undress.

She watched him, admiring his grace and the play of muscles under his skin as he drew the tunic over his head. His long hair stroked his back. Then she quietly exited the room and entered her own chamber and her waiting bath.

Until that moment, when he had shifted into the face of her daughter, it had never occurred to her that he would harm her or her loved ones. It had never occurred to her because she loved him, and she had thought herself incapable of loving a monster. Yet she did.

* * *

At precisely the ninth bell, Straif and AnnWyn were once more standing within the Council chamber. It was not yet their time to speak, which allowed Straif the opportunity to study the conversation and determine if he would be returning to Earth.

Of the five men who made up the Council, Straif decided that only Spindle Slan would object.

His mind had been unable to sleep, so he had spent the early morning hours deep in thought. The addition of that one woman he had seen with Ash changed all of his preconceived notions regarding the power of the House of Brendt. He was well aware of the network of loyalists that webbed throughout Ruis, plotting the demise of the House of Lophft. Many of his assignments were aimed at weakening that network.

But was there another network on Earth? Had the Brendt broken the Ruis code and elicited help from off-worlders? Or had they skillfully placed their own within the Earthean community? Straif smiled. It was a good idea, and something to be considered.

Was the woman from Brendt, and was she brought over by Ash to help him? But he knew Ash. Ash walked alone. Ash did not need help. Ash was, Straif begrudgingly admitted, as good a Walker as he was an Assassin. It was too bad, Straif reflected, they had such different loyalties. They would have made an unbeatable team.

And what of their father? Why had Theron not spoken of the woman? Was she unimportant, then? As Ambassador and Representative of the House of Brendt, Theron knew a great many of the clan's secrets.

Straif's mind lingered upon his father. Although he hated him, he could not help but admire the man. Theron used his gift of Charm as a warrior would wield a fine sword. The Council of Lophft knew that he was a spy, yet no one was able to produce the evidence needed for a trial and an execution.

It was dangerous to have a Brent spy in Lophft, yet when Straif pressed the Council to have him assassinated, he was always given the same negative response. Straif frowned. As Theron was of the royal bloodline of Brendt, he was a hostage as well as Ambassador. And, as Ogdan had explained on more than one occasion, no matter how accidental Theron's death might appear, there would be others who would question it. Lophft could not afford more people sympathizing with the Brendt. Even after two hundred years, there were too many loyalists. What the Council really needed from Theron was not his death, but rather the information contained within his mind.

In the end, it had been so easy. The Council had simply played upon Theron's weaknesses for drink and women. Although very careful about the women he chose, Theron was unaware that the latest girl who had caught his eye had a younger brother who had recently lost an eye and the little toe of his right foot. The girl had known just what to do to stop these "accidents." Straif smiled to himself. It had given him much amusement to shift his face into the features of the girl's brother when only she could see him. At times, he would make it appear as if the boy had two missing eyes.

Straif's thoughts returned to the Council room, and he studied the five men seated around the table. He knew they all thought him a necessary evil. None liked him, save, perhaps, Ogdan the Elder. That was fine with Straif. The position of Head Assassin did not bring friendship with it. And he did not much like the Council members, either.

Ogdan the Elder sat in the same chair in front of the fire as the night before. He was still draped in burgundy robes. It did not look as if he had slept, but Straif knew that Ogdan seldom slept for more than one or two hours a night. Many a night had he been summoned from his own bed to receive an assignment from the man.

To Ogdan's right sat Spindle Slan, smoothing out an imperfection on his tunic sleeve. Next to Spindle, sat Col Ailim, then Gor Andres. Moore of Lophft completed the circle. Only Ogdan the Elder and Moore were truly of the House of Lophft, though all Council members had Lophft blood flowing through their veins.

The five were hunched together, speaking in quiet tones. From time to time they glanced over at Straif.

He knew what they were thinking. They did not want him present. They did not think he belonged in that room. He knew too much about their decisions. He was brash and young. He was a killer who enjoyed his assignments.

But Straif was also both of the House of Lophft and of Brendt. He was unique. Councilman Moore's sister, Straif's highly ambitious mother, made sure that Theron had begotten a child with her. She had big plans for her son, and her mind was devious and sharp. Had she not been a woman, Estelle of Lophft would have been sitting in Moore's seat.

And Straif's lineage was useful to the Council. His name was linked with the Prophecy. Although the birth signs were not there, Straif had a great deal of clout in court. Many doors had been opened to him, and his mother had taught him how to use each opportunity.

Straif caught Spindle looking at him, and he held his gaze until Spindle looked down.

"And now we come to Straif," Ogdan the Elder began. "Straif has requested we release him from his last assignment and assign him the task of hunting down the woman from Earth, to discover what she knows."

"But we do not know if she is from Earth," Spindle pointed out in his dusty voice. His lank, dark hair had been woven with ribbons that matched the dark green of his tunic. He would have been considered handsome, but his chin lacked strength.

"No, we do not, Spindle. I simply named her that so we could know of whom we are speaking," Ogdan answered wearily.

"But the woman was carrying the child, was she not?" inquired Col Ailim. "Surely she will be with Ash when he arrives at the Brendt encampment. Our team of men will apprehend her."

Gor Andres leaned forward, his forearms on the table. "I agree with Col," he said. "Straif and his Walker should travel to the encampment, where he can finish his current assignment."

"I concur," agreed Moore.

The other Council members nodded in assent.

"Well, then, Straif," Ogdan said. "It seems that you have two assignments that take you, not to Earth, but to the Encampment of Brendt. I suggest you go straightaway."

"No!" Straif said vehemently.

The head Council member raised an eyebrow. "Indeed?"

The others muttered and glared at Straif.

Straif took a breath. He realized he would need to placate the Council if he were to get his way. His mother's voice purred from his memory "Give them honey, my sweet. It works wonders," she had told him often enough.

Straif tried to look contrite and bowed deeply to the five men. "Gentlemen," he began courteously. "I must apologize. I was rude and spoke out of turn. I can only defend my act by telling you that I am weary, having stayed awake this long night thinking about these events." He turned and spoke directly to Ogdan the Elder. "If you please, sir, might I defend my ignoble outburst?"

Ogdan nodded. "I accept the apology you have offered most eloquently to the Council. Please speak freely, as I am curious what thoughts this long night has visited upon you."

Straif bowed once more. "Thank you, sir."

He paused briefly, then leaned forward and rested his hands upon the Council table, making sure that he had the attention of all five men before continuing. "Thank you, gentlemen, for granting me this opportunity."

Straif paused again, then he spoke rapidly. "I ask you to recall my first assignment as Head Assassin of Lophft. As you remember, I was asked to destroy the smuggling network that was controlled by Smyther, the Merchant of Ambrose. Not only was Smyther one of the main suppliers of weapons, staples and information to the Brendt, he was also making himself very wealthy and very powerful by smuggling into Ruis collectable items from the Earth world and other worlds, but mainly from Earth. You know how we Ruisians are.

"My assignment took several months, as I needed to become familiar with Smyther's methods and to gain his trust." Straif smiled with satisfaction.

"Smyther only sent one man, Nox, with his Walker, to establish the trade networks. It was his strength, as well as his weakness. I destroyed the network by destroying Nox. According to code, the Walker lived." He glanced behind him where AnnWyn stood quietly, hands folded in front of her. "AnnWyn's knowledge of Earth is second only to Ash's. Together, we blend seamlessly into that environment."

"But what has this to do with your dispatch of a child and a woman who may or may not be of Earth?" Spindle blurted.

"Because, sir," Straif sneered, angered, "if Smyther could have a network of people unwittingly providing goods to Ruis, then why could not Ash of Brendt have a similar network? If I were one of the Brendt, I would have constructed just such an enterprise. The babe was sent to Earth to be hidden until he was of age. Who was going to oversee the child's safety as he grew? Truly, I feel we have underestimated Ash."

"But surely Theron would have known of these matters," countered Spindle.

"Not necessarily," Gor responded. "He is an ambassador, and although very good with using Charm, there has always been the possibility that he could be made to give us information. In fact, that is just what happened."

"And if I were of Brendt," continued Moore, "I would not tell my ambassador everything that I was plotting in order to protect myself from just such a scenario."

The head Councilman cleared his throat. "You make a good case for yourself, Straif," he said. "But why not conduct your, er, research after you have finished your assignment?"

Straif straightened, using his hands to accent his point. "Sir, you have sent a group of your elite to attack the Brendt encampment. It will soon be under our control and it will be easy for the elite to capture a woman and a babe. Simply separate them from the Walker.

"I see myself as a failsafe, just in case our plans for the encampment do not work out. A fox has two exits to its den. I will ensure that the other exit will be covered."

Ogdan the Elder clapped his hands. "You see, gentlemen, why we need Straif's attendance here? He is cunning itself!"

Straif kept his face impassive, but inside he was buoyant with joy, knowing he had just taken several major steps down the path he and his mother had envisioned for him.

He glanced over his shoulder. "Come, AnnWyn. We have work to do."

Chapter 6 – Plan B

With a gasp, Kate sat up in bed, suddenly awake. Memories came flooding into her consciousness. A tear slid down her cheek as she remembered the dying boy's eyes.

She angrily wiped her face and drew a shuddering breath as she realized that Joey's crying had waked her. She watched for a moment as Ash unsuccessfully tried to soothe the baby in his arms.

"Let me," she said.

Ash gratefully handed Joey to Kate. "I did not know you were awake. How are you, Kate?"

"I'm not sure," she replied. She placed Joey on the bed and reached for the diaper bag, glancing up at Ash. "He needs changing."

Ash watched her and then crossed over to look out the window as she finished up.

Kate rummaged around in the diaper bag and handed Joey a rubber duck for him to squeak. "We're going to have to get some baby supplies," she said to Ash's back. "We're pretty low."

She yawned and pushed the bangs off her face. "I really don't remember how we got back here," she said thoughtfully.

Ash crossed back to the bed and sat on its other side. Joey dropped his duck and crawled over to play with Ash's fingers. "You lost consciousness. I carried you and the babe back to this room." He glanced at her, smiling. "I had trouble masking us. It was difficult to carry you both."

"Masking? What do you mean?"

Ash searched for words. "We do not become invisible to others, exactly. But I can make it such that their minds slide over the fact that they are seeing us."

Kate was thoughtful. "I should thank you for taking care of us." She smiled wanly, her face paled. "I'm sorry I fell apart like that. It was horrible. He looked like a kid my age." She dug her fists into her eyes. "I keep seeing his face."

Ash let go of Joey and reached across the bed for her hands.

"Aye, it is horrible, that it is." He gently pulled her hands from her face. Kate could feel the strength in them and felt comforted. "Look at me, Kate."

She glanced up, ignoring the tears that threatened to spill down her cheeks.

Ash spoke slowly. "I need to know, Kate." His grip tightened slightly. "For the sake of the babe, could you do it again? Could you kill again?"

Kate looked down at their hands, then over at Joey, who was sitting up now, watching them. The baby gave her a solemn smile. "For Joey? I don't know, Ash," she whispered softly. "I just can't deal with this right now."

Ash nodded and gave her hands another squeeze before he released them. "I understand. But I will need an answer, Kate. Soon."

Kate continued to watch Joey. "I'm going to need some baby supplies," she repeated and glanced at the clock. Her eyes widened. "It's late! Why isn't Joey hungry?"

"While you slept, we went and ate pie."

"*Pie!* You can't give a baby pie for a meal!"

Ash laughed. "We ate soup first, then the pie."

Kate shook her head. "Men," she said smiling.

Ash returned her smile before sobering. "Kate, while you slept I devised a plan of which you are an important part. Can you help me for a little longer?"

Kate glanced at Joey and then back to Ash. She wondered if the baby would look like Ash when he was grown. With their dark hair and green eyes, they already could pass for father and son.

"Does everyone from the House of Brendt look the same?"

Ash blinked and his expression went blank. "Yes, there is a strong resemblance among us. But Kate, will you help me?"

Kate laughed. "I'm sorry. My thoughts keep jumping around. Yes I will help you a while longer. But I need to let my parents know what's going on. They must be really worried by now. Heck, they probably think *I'm* dead. It's not fair to them. It hurts, thinking how upset they probably are."

Ash shook his head sadly. "I cannot allow that to happen just yet. But soon, I promise you."

Disappointed, Kate sighed. "Well then, what is your plan?"

"It is simple. We must find a safe place, and Ruis is not safe until I discover the whereabouts of my Kinsmen.

"Therefore, we remain here, on Earth. Once we find a safe place, then I can leave Ioho under your protection while I return to Ruis and locate my Kinsmen. That is why I asked if you could kill again, Kate. There is the possibility that you may need to do it in order to save his life."

Kate nodded in understanding. "But who would I be killing?"

"Those seeking to kill Ioho," Ash answered.

He would not meet her glance. Kate watched him, puzzled. Then her eyes widened. "Omigod, you're talking about Straif! He the one who is after Joey! You think I can kill a trained assassin? He'll murder us both!"

Ash held up a hand. "Let me speak further, Kate. My plan does not include your death, believe me. Will you listen without interruption?"

Ash waited for her nod before he continued. "On Ruis, trees are very sacred. After all, they are portals into other worlds. And what is most sacred is a cluster of trees that grows in a semicircle. Within that semicircle, a person is unharmed for as long as he remains within its boundary. If we can find such a place, we will be safe. And, when I leave to search for my Kinsmen, you and Ioho will be safe as well. Not even Straif will break that law. The law is a part of our very beings."

He paused to see if Kate understood what he was telling her.

"And I will not just leave you the moment we find this place. I will stay for as long as it takes for me to teach you what I know of Straif: his fighting techniques, his methods, his strengths and weaknesses. We will practice together. Upon my life, Kate, you will be prepared.

"And when you are ready, I will not just leave you and Ioho and seek my Kinsmen. I will leave and return, and leave and return. I will be gone no more than two or three days at a time; whatever makes you feel the most safe."

Ash stopped and waited for Kate to speak. The hotel room was quiet, save for the muffled sounds of traffic. Even Joey had stopped his playing, eyes fastened upon Kate, who was staring out into the fading afternoon light.

Kate watched a gull glide towards the bay. "You've put a lot of thought into this, haven't you?"

"That I have, Kate."

She looked at Ash. "And you will train me?"

"Aye, with the sword. You say you know some techniques already. We will build upon those. You will see."

"And how do you know so much about Straif?"

Ash looked down at his hands resting on his thighs. Then he glanced back at Kate. "I did not think you needed to know."

"But?" asked Kate.

"But, there should be no secrets between us for trust to grow. So, I will tell you. Straif is my half-brother. We have the same father."

Kate's eyes widened. "Hold on. Straif is on the side of the House of Lophft, right?" Ash nodded. "Then, how come you're on two different sides? I don't get it."

Ash smiled sadly. "It is not confusing if you know the full story, and I see that you need to know."

Ash sat back, leaning against the headboard and folding his arms. "We will begin with my father. My father's name is Theron, and he is a nobleman from the House of Brendt. He is also Brendt's ambassador with Lophft and lives most of the year in Phaelon, the capital city of Ruis. Lophft also has an ambassador who resides with us in one of our strongholds." Ash smiled slightly. "It is how we keep each other in line. Ambassadors are also hostages."

Ash crossed his legs. "And ambassadors are also spies. Everyone knows this, but they cannot be named a spy unless they are caught doing so.

"Now, my father's gift is that of Charm. He can get you to tell him your innermost secrets without you realizing you are even doing it. In fact, he can talk his way out of any situation. It is an amazing thing to witness. Charm is a perfect gift to have if you are an ambassador, hostage and spy." Ash grinned. "It is also a very good gift to have if you enjoy the ladies. And my father enjoys ladies very much." Ash put a hand over his heart. "Kate, if you were ever to meet my father, I promise I would never leave you alone in the same room with him. You have my word on that!"

Not knowing how serious Ash was being, Kate smiled "I think I get what you mean. Go on."

"Several years ago, when I was young, my father convinced the Council of the House of Lophft that, as an ambassador, he should be allowed to return to his home from time to time. However, as a hostage, my father would need to remain at Lophft. Therefore, he suggested (and it was accepted) that, as Theron's son, I would make a suitable hostage. So, for four months out of the year, I lived at Lophft.

"It was then that I got to know Straif. Straif befriended me." Ash's eyes grew distant. "I did think we were friends. I was very happy being with him. He was older and I looked up to him. I never knew until long afterwards how much Straif despised me."

"*Why?*" asked Kate.

"Because I was my father's son and of Brendt. Straif hates the House of Brendt. I fear his mother has poisoned his mind."

"I'm so sorry, Ash."

"Oh, it was long ago, Kate. I was a boy. And my memories are happy ones. Before Straif told the Council I was a Walker, we had many adventures. But after that I was forced to leave. Walkers make poor hostages," he commented wryly. "My father found someone with a more suitable gift to be the four-month hostage."

Kate laughed, glancing at the clock by the bed. "Hey! It's getting late. Why don't we get some dinner? I'm hungry."

Ash hesitated. "I do not think that is a good idea. You are considered dead and your name and picture are in the newspapers."

Kate's smile vanished. "Then how can I buy supplies for us? Joey needs some things. We're running low on diapers, and he'll need new clothes."

"Many of these items I can acquire from Ruis. Also, I can mask you for a short while. It takes great mental effort. May I suggest we order food and have it delivered to our room? After we have eaten and it is less crowded outside, we can purchase necessities. The store across the way says it is never closed."

* * *

It was dark when the three crossed the hotel parking lot, heading for the Ray's Food Mart that was next to the hotel. Earlier Ash had procured a baseball cap which Kate used to hide her hair. Kate shifted the backpack which housed a sleeping Joey into a more comfortable position.

"I was thinking about your Cathedral of Trees," she said.

Ash glanced at her. "Cathedral of Trees?"

"Yes, it's what you described: the semicircle of trees? Anyway, redwoods grow like that. There's a place deep in the forest around here called the Headwaters. It's filled with old growth redwoods, ancient trees, some more than a thousand years old. I've only been there once. It's protected by the government and not many people go there. It takes all day to hike up, and it's a difficult trail. But, for you it'd be easy."

Ash's eyes lit up. "What you describe sounds perfect. I will need a map so that I can picture it in my mind. But it should be easy to find. Trees as ancient as the ones you describe speak to me. I can find them with my soul." He glanced at Kate. "This is very good news," he said warmly. "I thank you, Kate."

Kate smiled and ducked under the brim of her baseball cap so Ash could not see her blush.

"I'll just get a few items from my list. If I keep out of sight, you'll only need to mask me during the checkout process."

Ash scanned the area. "Do you see that tree by the red building halfway to the hotel? If there is trouble, it will be our portal."

"Okay, Ash. But you worry too much. Nobody I know shops at Ray's at 1:00 in the morning."

But Kate was wrong.

Chapter 7 – Time to Go

AnnWyn released Straif's arm as soon as they had crossed through the final portal. It was mid-morning and the fog that had shrouded Eureka all night was just lifting. Straif looked about. He could smell the burnt wood.

"Why here, AnnWyn?"

AnnWyn glanced up at him. He had changed his features so that they were softer, less striking. He was dressed in a plaid cotton shirt over a t-shirt and jeans, with sweatshirt tied at his waist. The black backpack he carried held his weapons and additional clothing.

AnnWyn pushed back the hood of her Walker's cloak and shook out her hair. Although she wore her cloak, she had masked herself and appeared to be dressed in jeans and a t-shirt that read "Old Navy" on the front. "I did not know where else to go," she answered. "This part of the Earth is unfamiliar to me, and I have not closely studied your map. You will need to allow me the time to do so if I am to be of better assistance."

Straif glanced at her, shrugged off his backpack, rummaged around in it and withdrew a map of the area. Together, they looked it over.

"We need lodgings," Straif stated.

"Then I suggest we go here," AnnWyn pointed. "It looks like a main thoroughfare. There should be plenty of inns from which to choose."

"Then let's begin." Straif refolded the map and stashed it in his pack, then swung the pack over one shoulder as they started off in the direction AnnWyn had indicated. As they walked, Straif began to plot his strategy, but AnnWyn broke into his thoughts.

"Who is the babe, Straif?" she asked quietly.

He glanced at her, surprised. "You do not know?"

She shook her head. "But the situation must be important, as I have never participated in a meeting when all five Council members were present."

Straif glanced at her. "And?" he prompted.

"I did not say 'and,'" she replied, confused.

"There was no need. There is more to your query, is there not?"

AnnWyn sighed. "*And*," she stressed the word, stopping to face him, "it has been your custom to tell me of your missions."

Straif studied AnnWyn as she looked up at him. Compared with his mother and other women he had known, she was plain. Her hair was a nondescript brown, her face square, lips thin, eyes large. Yet there was something about her that was so very attractive. Maybe it was those wide-set hazel eyes. She had the look of a Walker: eyes that had seen other places, other worlds. She was separate from others, as was he. Perhaps it was kinship he felt.

He had changed things between them when he had threatened her. He knew it would never be the same for her, could tell that he had wounded her deeply. Did it bother him, he wondered? He did not know. He had not permitted himself to think about it.

AnnWyn coughed. Straif had been staring at her for so long that she was beginning to get nervous.

"The babe is Ioho," he said.

AnnWyn gasped. "How can that be?"

"The signs are as they were foretold. The Prophecy has been fulfilled by his birth."

AnnWyn was silent, absorbing the information. "Then, it has begun. The birth of Ioho marks the Golden Age of Ruis." She looked up again at Straif. "If you kill this babe, he will not unite all of Ruis under one benevolent kingdom. There would be no Golden Age if he were to die."

"If he does not die, AnnWyn, there will no longer be a House of Lophft."

"But he is just a babe!"

"It is easier to kill him as a babe."

AnnWyn gasped, her eyes looking even larger against the stark white of her face. "But you have never killed a child before!"

"I have never been asked to do so before."

She reached a hand out but hesitated to touch him. "I cannot help you with this, Straif. I cannot be a part of this killing."

Straif's face hardened as he looked at her. "Do not say such things, AnnWyn." His voice was tight as he held back his anger.

"Don't you *see*, Straif? Ruis needs this Golden Age. You are not just killing a child! You would be killing the future of Ruis!"

"Ruis has a future. The House of Lophft will continue to govern, and things will remain as they are."

"But they cannot! Life is so unbalanced on Ruis. There are the very rich and the very poor. I know what it is like to be of the very poor."

Straif scowled. "I have an assignment, AnnWyn, that is all."

"It is *not* all, Straif!"

Straif grabbed her arm and squeezed it painfully. "Are you willing to trade the life of your daughter for the life of an unknown babe?" he asked, flinging her arm away.

AnnWyn took a step back. Her hand came slowly up to cover her mouth which had formed a silent O. Straif held her gaze until she lowered her eyes and silently shook her head.

"Then let us not speak of this nonsense again." And he began walking away.

Head down, AnnWyn silently followed.

* * *

Kate stood in the baby aisle looking at the contents of her cart, trying to determine if she had enough baby wipes, when she felt a hand tentatively touch her shoulder. She turned, expecting Ash, and came face to face with John Sullivan, Joey's father. Her surprise was echoed on his face.

"Kate?" He glanced at the sleeping baby strapped to her back. "Joey?" Joey's eyes flew open at the sound of his name. "What is this? Kate? Wha—!"

Not knowing what else to do, Kate bolted with Joey.

Behind her, Mr. Sullivan had begun to run after her, shouting. His cries brought more and more people to his aid, and others began to chase Kate.

Dodging a shopping cart, Kate focused on the main door of the grocery.

"Lock the doors!" someone commanded. To Kate's horror, she saw the large glass doors sliding closed.

"Quickly, take my hand, Kate!" Ash said as he suddenly appeared at her side.

Together, they burst through the glass doors. Kate felt a momentary chill. Had they just run through the doors? The sensation was so brief that she could not tell. She tried to look behind her and stumbled, nearly falling. Ash caught her.

"Run, Kate!" he commanded. "The tree by the red building—faster now!"

Kate focused on her goal. She heard a police siren from behind. And then another. *How had the police gotten there so fast? And why had Ash picked a tree so far away from them?*

Kate ran faster, the police floodlights casting their shadows in front of them. Joey began to squeal with laughter, and the police were saying something to them over their speaker system.

Ash yanked her towards the tree and she nearly stumbled again. "Jump!" he shouted.

Kate jumped after Ash, one hand clasped in his, the other out bracing for a fall, but Ash kept pulling her. In one step, they were in the Place-Between-Worlds, and in the next she was being pulled through another tree. Ash stopped so abruptly that she slammed into him.

He caught her before she could fall. They stood looking at each other, panting. Then Ash glanced behind her and grinned broadly at Joey.

"What?" Kate asked. She reached back and felt the baby's little fingers grasp her own.

"I think young Ioho was enjoying himself," Ash replied.

Joey burbled enthusiastically.

Kate gave the baby's fingers a light squeeze before she let go of his hand. "Joey, you are one adventurous little boy," she said.

Kate looked around enjoying the silence of the trees.

"That was close," she said.

"Aye, Kate, that it was."

"I wonder where we are," she murmured.

They were standing on a slope surrounded by redwoods. The trees were thick and tall, blotting out most of the sky. As her eyes adjusted to the dark, she noted that they were on a path of woodchips.

"I was hoping that we were near a Cathedral of Trees," Ash answered. "I reached out with my soul, and these trees answered me." He touched the tree he had used as a portal. His touch was gentle.

Kate squinted in concentration. "No, this isn't the Headwaters. The trees are too small. It seems familiar, though. Can we take this path a little way? Maybe I'll recognize something."

"I will follow you, Kate." Ash replied.

She paused before deciding to walk uphill. A short while later, the trail leveled off and then widened. When it intersected with pavement she stopped. "Okay, I know where we are. We're in Sequoia Park, behind the zoo."

"Then this is not the place you were describing," Ash shut his eyes in concentration. For a few moments there was silence. Then Ash's eyes flew open as he sucked in his breath. "The Grandfathers! I have found them Kate!"

Once more he took her hand and they strode towards the closest redwood. Kate paused and looked up its massive trunk, craning her neck back in order to see the top. "Now this is my idea of a portal," she said.

Ash smiled and they stepped through.

Chapter 8 – The Grandfathers

The first thing that Kate noticed as they stepped through from the Place-Between-Worlds was the silence. It was almost complete, far away from the undertone of traffic that was always present in the city. It awed her and made her feel small and insignificant. It overwhelmed her as well, and made her long for her parents, her home and her bedroom.

"Kate?" She started and glanced over at Ash, wide-eyed. "What troubles you, Kate?"

His concern made her feel a little better and she gave him a small smile. "It's just that I've never felt so far away from people before. It's so quiet. Not even a barking dog." She looked around at the tall, massive shapes of the trees looming far over her head. She shivered. "And I miss my Mom and Dad," she said, her voice wobbling.

"You are so brave, Kate, that I forget how it must truly be for you. I am sorry. Please, do not fear this place, Kate. Can you not feel the peace of the Grandfathers? Here…" He reached for her hand and placed it upon the ancient bark of the nearest redwood. "Let it give you its strength."

Kate closed her eyes and breathed in the atmosphere of the place. Her heightened senses absorbed the quiet, making it an ally rather than an enemy to her peace of mind. She exhaled and began to relax, feeling her fears drain away. She felt safe and hidden from her pursuers. It felt to her as if the tree had taken on all that had happened to her, sharing her burden. The events of the past two days were not as terrifying. She blinked. *Had it only been two days?*

"Better?"

Kate smiled. "Yes."

63

"See where we stand, Kate."

Still maintaining her contact with the tree, Kate looked about. They were standing within a semicircle of redwoods, so large that their sides nearly touched at the back where the semicircle arched around.

"A Cathedral of Trees," she breathed.

"Aye. Sanctuary."

They stood for a few moments in silence. Kate leaned her head back, watching the stars through the boughs. "So, what next, Ash?"

"Let us rest and then plan when it's light. We have time now. Within these Grandfathers we will be well hidden."

Joey sighed as Kate withdrew him from the backpack and laid him on a bed of pine needles wrapped in Ash's cloak. He snuggled into the softness and was asleep immediately.

Kate used her sweater as a pillow and lay down beside Joey.

She did not think she would sleep, but, to her surprise, it was a shaft of sunlight that woke her.

Yawning, she sat up and pulled her braid in front of her, absently picking out the redwood needles and wondering where to find a bathroom.

"Hello, she-who-sleeps-the-day-away." Ash was seated not far from her with his back against a tree and his arms folded. His sword lay across his lap. He looked alert and at home. His smile was dazzling.

"Have you been awake long?" she asked. His eyes seemed so green in the morning light.

"Long enough to make a plan." He nodded towards the opening of the semicircle. "Around that way is a private spot to take care of any necessities."

"Thanks," she replied. Glancing at Joey, who still was asleep, Kate rose and went to relieve herself.

On her way back, she paused at the edge of a meadow, feeling the warmth of the sun on her shoulders. The harsh cry of a Jay overshadowed the lighter songbirds. A Tiger Swallowtail flitted across the clearing.

Ash strode over to stand beside her. He raised his arms, clasping his hands behind his head. "This is a fine meadow in which to practice, do you not agree?"

Kate looked at him questioningly and he continued. "You would not want your practice area to be too flat, as it would not be authentic." He gestured at the meadow with his head. "The ground is fairly even here, and there is plenty of area to swing a blade without injury."

Kate looked at the gentle slope as it ran down towards another grove of trees. "I wish I had my *bokuto,*" she murmured. A flash of silver caught her eye. "Say, isn't that a creek down there?"

"Aye, it is so, and the water is truly sweet."

Kate shot a look at him. "How long have you been up, really?"

Ash laughed. "Not long. Long enough to explore a bit." He turned and looked up towards the Cathedral of Trees where Joey still slept. "I do not believe we will have to relocate. This area is perfect for our needs."

Kate followed his gaze. "Can't someone sneak up on us from that way?"

"It is a possibility, but the underbrush is nice and thick and will make noise. And I will place some traps and snares around our sanctuary." He glanced at her. "I will show you where they are, but you will still need to be cautious," he said seriously. "Better still, perhaps I shall teach you how to make the traps yourself"

Kate nodded and her stomach growled. "Yikes! I guess I'm hungrier than I thought!" she exclaimed.

"I have food for us, and some supplies. I went back to Eureka while you slept."

Kate's eyes widened and then narrowed as she scowled. "But you said you would not leave us alone. What if I'd waked up? I would have freaked!" she scolded.

Ash bowed slightly, his eyes twinkling. "Forgive me, Kate. You did not look as if either you or Ioho would awaken any time soon." He sobered. "Remember, Kate, you were safe in the sanctuary of the Grandfathers. I was not gone long. Truly," he added softly.

Kate sighed. "I should trust you more. Let's eat, okay? I'm hungry and cranky."

Returning to their shelter of trees, they found Joey awake, sitting up in his nest and about to crawl out. He gave them a happy squeal. Over a breakfast of fruit, yogurt and chunks of bread, Ash told Kate what he had learned while he was in town.

The news was all over town that Kate had been spotted. The mystery of there being two Joeys had caused much excitement and speculation. The police were determined to find Kate for questioning. Mr. Sullivan was sure that she had the true Joey and the other baby was an imposter. There was talk of DNA testing. Kate's parents had issued a plea for Kate to come forward. They were just as confused as everyone else.

"Oh Ash," Kate moaned. "My poor Mom and Dad! Please take me to them!" she begged.

Ash looked at her and sadly shook his head. "I cannot, Kate. When Ioho has been delivered, when he is safe—not until then, Kate."

She looked at Ash miserably. "I just can't have them so worried about me." A tear slid down her cheek. "I really need to see them. They need to know. Can't you just take me right into the house? It's all wood and there's a huge stone fireplace in our living room."

"I understand your pain. I do. But I cannot risk this. Please do not ask this of me."

"But I *have* to ask, Ash! I need them to know that I have done nothing wrong and that I am all right!"

"Kate, they will want explanations that I am not willing to give," he explained quietly. "You must understand that you are an exception. Those from Ruis traveling off-world never reveal themselves."

Joey had stopped eating and had crawled into Kate's lap.

"And there is Ioho," he continued. "The babe is our future, our hope. His safety must come first."

Kate hugged Joey to her, burying her face in his soft curls. Her bangs slid forward and covered her face. She did not bother to brush them back. She sat in silence for several moments, gently rocking the baby, allowing him to play with her braid.

"*Very well*," Ash spoke vehemently.

Startled, Kate looked up, her eyes bright with unshed tears. *Why was he so angry?*

"In a week's time I will take you to see your mother and father. But I will survey the area first, and I will take you only if your dwelling is safe to my satisfaction. It is against my better judgment, but this I will do for you." He glowered at her.

Brushing away her thanks, he continued. "Tell me the additional items you need for the babe and for yourself," he said briskly as he rose to his feet. "I will acquire these things. And then I will make this area safe."

Chapter 9 – Not Good

Straif turned off the television and threw the remote control onto his bed in disgust. AnnWyn glanced up at him mildly from where she sat reading the daily newspaper.

"That was very foolish of Ash," he exclaimed. "But it appears that my brother and this maiden slipped through the net the Council cast." He grinned. "They will remember how it was *my* idea to come back to Earth. Now to catch them."

Straif began to pace. "If I were Ash, what would I do next?" he mused. "Where would I go?"

He fell silent as he thought about his brother. What *were* Ash's options? "If *I* were Ash…" He paused, then continued speaking slowly, "I would want to get the babe to safety as quickly as possible." Straif glanced at AnnWyn. "I am going to assume that Ash came upon the Brendt encampment, and that he found it surrounded by Lophft men-at-arms. And he obviously returned here to Earth. Now then, surely Ash has other strongholds. I doubt we know all of them. But why did he not go there? There must be some sort of holdup."

Straif glanced at AnnWyn to ensure that he had her attention. "Knowing my cautious little brother as I do, I would wager he would find a safe place to hide the babe while he sought information. I would further wager that my brother would not hide the babe on Ruis."

He raised his eyes in thought. "As a Walker, I could hide the babe wherever there were trees. Therefore, if I were Ash, I would hide the babe right here, amongst the network of sympathizers that I have created.

"Ash would be unaware that I saw him with the woman—a child watcher—how clever. Therefore, the best place for us to locate my missing brother and his charge would be at that woman's dwelling."

"You call the child watcher a 'woman?'" AnnWyn asked as she held up the newspaper. "She is a maiden, living with her parents. And further, it reads that the parents do not know what has happened to their daughter. They had assumed she had died in the fire while rescuing the babe."

"What they say means nothing," replied Straif. "And, if it pleases you, I shall call her a maiden. What is important to remember is what the *maiden's* parents say and what they know are two very different things. I will find out what they know. Can you take me to their dwelling?"

AnnWyn nodded.

"Well, then, it is time I went to work."

* * *

AnnWyn glanced at Straif. She had seen him impersonate others countless times, but it never ceased to amaze her how he could instantly take on not only a person's likeness, but their mannerisms as well.

She knew other shape-shifters. They could usually be found in traveling theatrical troupes or living as thieves. Although they could always impersonate others, compared to Straif, they were amateurs. AnnWyn assumed that it must be Straif's intelligence. No matter how much one could look like another person, it took intelligence and an acute sense of observation to be able to behave like that person as well.

AnnWyn sighed as she glanced at Straif. All of the fight had gone out of her. She knew and accepted that she loved the monster that was Straif. She felt that the phrase "follow to hell and back," which she had picked up from her travels, summed up what she would do for this man. She just hoped that someday he would understand that about her and reciprocate her feelings. But she doubted it.

Studying Straif as they sat together in the squad car, AnnWyn could tell that impersonating Officer Small was very taxing for him. He was placing himself in an environment of which he possessed very little knowledge. She helped him, of course, by cloaking herself and accompanying him, so that she could share her knowledge of Earthian society and structure. Selecting an officer with a dog as his partner was a wise move.

AnnWyn looked at the dog Rocky panting in the back seat of the car. How Straif had gotten that dog to accept him, she never knew. Perhaps he had inherited some of his father's Charm, she thought ruefully. It would explain a great deal.

She looked back at Straif, who must have felt her gaze.

"I have been thinking," he said in the raspy tenor of the officer. "I do not think we will be needing Officer Small much longer. I think that it is time to pay the Johnsons one more visit. Afterwards, Officer Small can be found in his car." Straif smiled. "One more mystery for them to solve," he murmured.

"What do you hope to discover during this last visit?"

"I think it is time to become the father."

AnnWyn kept the tension out of her voice. "And why is that?"

"This test that they gave the babe…what is its name?"

"The DNA test?"

"Aye, that is it," Straif replied, allowing a trace of his accent to show.

The dog whined and Straif glanced at it in the rearview mirror. "Sorry, Rocky!" he said in Small's voice. "It has been nearly a week" he continued to AnnWyn, "and the results will show that the babe is their own. When that occurs, the interest will no longer be focused on the maiden and her parents. I believe that Ash and the girl will show themselves at that time. I plan to be already in place."

Straif studied AnnWyn. "When you cloak yourself, would you be able to make your hair a lighter color? I believe the mother's hair is a little lighter than yours."

AnnWyn shook her head. "I cannot change my features or hair color. There is a chemical I can use to change the hair color."

Straif nodded. "We will do what we can." He reached for his officer's hat, glanced at himself in the mirror, and made a minor adjustment. "Give me half an hour. If I am not back, come and get me. Stay, Rocky."

Less than twenty minutes later a rather grim Officer Small returned to his car. Straif glanced at AnnWyn as he jabbed the key into the ignition. He was silent as he turned the car on and put it in gear. He reached into a pocket inside his jacket and drew out a lock of hair, handing it to AnnWyn. "Here is the color you must match. We will relocate ourselves tonight."

AnnWyn accepted the lock and wrapped it in a tissue for safekeeping. Rocky whined. "I think Rocky needs to be walked," AnnWyn commented.

Straif nodded as he headed back to the police station. "I will be glad when I am no longer Officer Small," he said.

He glanced at AnnWyn, frustration darkening his features. "I am truly baffled, AnnWyn. I do not know what Ash is thinking. There is no House of Brendt network here on Earth. I was wrong."

* * *

"Daddy!"

Straif barely had time to compose his features when the front door was flung open and the girl was in his arms. He instantly recognized the baby in the backpack she was wearing.

It was all so easy, he thought as his arms tightened about the girl.

She pulled back and looked at him, her face glowing. "Oh Daddy! I've missed you and Mom so much! I'm so sorry that I couldn't get here sooner, but," she glanced behind her, "Ash thought we should wait until things died down." She took a deep breath and let it out. "But now I can tell you everything!" she exclaimed happily. "Don't be mad at me, okay?"

71

Straif cleared his throat. "How could I be angry at my own child?" he asked.

Straif felt her body stiffen. What was wrong, he wondered. He wanted her relaxed, unsuspecting, as he decided how to quickly grab the baby from where he sat just inches away. He glanced at his prey. Their eyes locked. *Those eyes! What power behind those eyes!* A chill went up Straif's spine. Unconsciously he whispered, "Ioho."

The girl in his arms gasped, ducked out of his embrace with a side step as she punched both her fists into his gut.

"You're not my Dad!" she shouted.

Out of nowhere Straif, doubled over in pain, watched his brother, his sword drawn, move between him and his target. Straif watched him hesitate and then quickly turn, grabbing the girl's hand and drawing her behind him towards the huge stone fireplace that dwarfed the living room.

Straif's eyes widened as he watched the three escape into the portal Ash had made of the fireplace. The last image of them disappearing was of two fearless and shining eyes as the babe once again gazed upon him. Then, with one hand over his belly, he called for AnnWyn.

AnnWyn burst into the room, looking wildly about. She started towards Straif, but he pointed at the stone fireplace.

"After them. AnnWyn! You must follow them! Quickly!"

"Where?" she asked.

"Ash made a portal of those stones! Now, *go!*"

"But that is impossible," she replied.

"*What?* " Straif's eyes blazed as his features blended back into his own.

"A Walker can only use the living tree as a portal," AnnWyn stated. "Only trees," she repeated.

"Well, the Walker that is Ash used *that*," he pointed at the fireplace, "as a portal. Now go after them! Quickly!" he roared. "Before the trail cools!"

AnnWyn crossed over to the fireplace and put her hand on the cold, rough stone. She closed her eyes briefly and then dropped her hand to her side. Taking a breath she turned back towards Straif. "I-I cannot do this. I do not understand how he did it," she said quietly, head lowered.

Straif stuttered with rage, his face growing red. "Y-you *dare* to disobey me? Go, AnnWyn! Just go through!"

"And if I lose my way, what then, Straif?"

Straif looked at her blankly.

"Who will come to you and take you back to Ruis if I am lost or killed?"

"*By the Book!*" Straif screamed, a vein throbbing at his temple. Scooping up a clay figurine, he hurled it at the fireplace. As AnnWyn ducked out of its path, the figurine shattered, sending fragments in all directions.

Wiping his hands on his borrowed shirtfront, Straif glanced at AnnWyn. He silently watched her dust the clay fragments off her robe and from her hair. "Aye, you are correct. It is time we leave this place."

* * *

Ash led Kate through the portal and into the Place-Between-Worlds. Kate felt she was walking through glue. Her lungs hurt from holding her breath. When they burst through, they both stumbled to their knees.

Kate opened her eyes. Ash and she were kneeling on a high, rocky plateau next to an outcropping of dusty, grey rock. The atmosphere was quiet and still.

"Where are we?" she asked.

Ash re-sheathed his sword and helped Kate to her feet. "We are in the Place-Between-Worlds," he answered. "But where, exactly, I do not know."

Kate shivered. "It feels creepy. Where are all the trees?"

Ash turned towards the rock from which they had emerged. His boots crunched on the loose gravel. He puts his hand on the rough surface. "I have never seen this place," he murmured. He closed his eyes and gazed inwardly, searching for the route back to their camp.

"Shouldn't we be going soon?" Kate asked after a few minutes. "I need to..." she stopped, searching for the right words, but they did not come. She shrugged, looking away. "I need to deal with all this," she said in a shaky voice.

Ash's glance was filled with compassion. "I do not know this place," he said again, looking around, eyes searching for signs of the danger he sensed drawing nearer. Instinctively, he stepped closer to Kate and Joey, his hand gripping his scabbard.

"This has never happened before," he said. "I cannot feel the path." Ash took a breath to calm himself. The danger was nearer, of that he was sure.

Joey gurgled and shoved a chubby fist into Ash's line of vision, startling him out of his thoughts. Annoyed, Ash reached to bat the tiny fist out of his face, but he paused when he saw what Joey was holding. Ash searched Joey's solemn face, then reached out to take the few redwood twigs from the baby's grasp.

"The Grandfathers!" Ash's eyes lit up. "This may be enough for me to reach them."

"Ohmigod! Ash! Above us!" Kate shrieked, her eyes fixed upon a horror only she had noticed. She reached up and held Joey's arm.

Kate's cry galvanized Ash into action.

"Do not let go," he commanded as he faded into the rock wall, fingers laced with Kate's.

When the three finally stepped through the Grandfather portal, Ash was bathed in sweat. What seemed mere moments to Kate had felt like an eternity to him. With his back leaning against the familiar bark of the trees, he gulped a deep breath of air.

Ash's eyes were glazed as he watched Kate and Joey. He wiped his face with the back of his sleeve.

"I did not think we would make it," he said. "I have moved through rock and water, but never rock alone before today." He studied Joey as Kate removed him from his carrier. "I do not pretend to understand how the babe knew, but those few twigs he held were all that saved us from certain death. Could he be a Walker as well?"

But Kate was not listening as she cradled the baby.

"Ash?" she asked. Her lip trembled. "My parents? Are they…?"

Ash's expression mirrored her own, and he quickly crossed over to her and gathered the girl and the baby into his embrace. "I do not hold much hope for them, Kate. It breaks my heart to tell you this. Tomorrow I will go back and learn the truth."

Kate's whole body began to shake. She felt like there were knives twisting in her gut and in her heart. "If…if they are..." Kate made herself say the word, "dead, then I am all alone."

Ash's grip tightened. "That is untrue, Kate. You have us."

Chapter 10 – TinneHolm

The shrill cry of the Steller's Jay echoed in the stillness of the early morning. Kate opened her eyes, sensing that something was not quite right. It was too still.

Slowly and silently she crept out of her blankets in the far corner of the lean-to she and Ash had made within the protective semicircle of the Grandfathers. She peered out into the early dawn gloom, her eyes widening with horror and incomprehension.

On the ground, near the opening, lay Ash, his long dark hair strewn about his body, the ends reddened with his blood. Next to him lay Joey, his sightless eyes staring, his neck slit.

She stifled a scream and a figure she had not noticed turned to look at her. It was her father! How could that be? He raised a bloodied sword above his head and strode towards her. She stood, intending to run, but his cold gaze froze her in place.

"I thought you would like to see a friendly face before you met your death," Straif said. "I have one last thing to do, and then I can return to my home, and the Prophecy will be no more."

Kate watched the sword's descent. Her last thoughts were, *Why am I giving up without a fight?* The last sound she heard was Straif's laughter.

* * *

Kate sat up, drenched in sweat. She reached for her *bokuto* and stepped into the morning quiet. The sun would not be up for another hour or so, but Kate knew she would be unable to sleep again. She couldn't, after that dream, and it was occurring more and more frequently.

"If I keep dreaming that thing for much longer, I'll never be able to sleep," she muttered. "I'm going to start looking like a raccoon."

Kate had taken enough psychology to realize why she was having the dream. The stress from the past two months was bound to reveal itself in some manner. It made her feel helpless, and that made her feel angry.

Since Joey had begun to crawl, they had gotten in the habit of putting his sleeping nest within a playpen Ash had found. Making sure that Joey was sleeping soundly and the pen's gate was closed, Kate strode to the center of the clearing-turned-training ground. She took her *bokuto* in her two hands, centered her mind, and began to practice. She paid attention to the first few swings, analyzing the cut line and cutting in different degrees along the vector that Ash had showed her.

But then, she let the rhythm of the swings relax her, and allowed her mind to wander.

It had been nearly seven weeks since Ash had brought back proof, in the form of a newspaper, that her parents were dead. The speculation surrounding their "double suicide" and her own whereabouts sickened her and filled her with grief. If it had not been for her need to care for Joey and Ash's relentless sword practices, Kate felt she would surely have fallen apart.

But her mind was strong, and she was disciplined. She locked up her feelings in the recesses of her mind and focused on the task at hand. She would examine her feelings later.

Kate had been surprised at her sword training. The first day of her practice, Ash had asked her to show him what she knew. As she stepped into *mugamae* to begin the techniques of the *Kihon Tachi* , he stopped her with a smile.

"I know this sword style," he had announced.

"But how?" she had asked.

"Later. Now we will practice."

Ash had taken her through all the lists of techniques she had learned, including spear and *naginata* techniques.

"I know I don't know much," Kate had apologized.

"But you know the important part," Ash had replied. "You know how to move with your sword."

He had put her through countless drills to train her to focus on reading her opponent. "First you must know what your enemy is going to do, Kate. You must be able to read his actions and to sense what his next move will be. When you can do that, you must then control his moves." He had laughed at her expression. "It is true, Kate. When you can read what he is about to do, you will then be able to control the outcome. And when you can control the outcome, you can control your enemy."

At the time Kate had been doubtful of her ability master what Ash had wanted her to learn. But as the weeks progressed and the hours of practice rolled by, she began to realize that she was anticipating more and more of Ash's attacks. Her confidence grew and, with that, her skill.

The days had fallen into an easy pattern. Upon waking, Kate usually went to the practice field while Joey slept and Ash disappeared into a portal for supplies and information. He was always searching for signs of Straif. Ash had told Kate that, knowing the assassin's skills, it was only a matter of time before their sanctuary was discovered.

Upon Ash's return, the three of them would eat breakfast, followed by more training, followed by lunch, followed by more training. At night, they would relax and play with Joey until his bedtime.

The afternoon training was Kate's favorite, as one of them would be carrying Joey in the backpack. Every time they would dodge and weave, Joey would begin to let out peals of laughter. His laughter was so infectious that soon all three would be laughing, and then they would have to stop, regain their focus, and begin again, only to have the cycle repeat itself until Joey's nap time.

At night, when Joey was safely asleep, Ash and Kate would sit together by the fire and tell each other about their pasts. Kate told Ash about her childhood and her hopes for success in gymnastics. As she told the story, she realized that now it all felt so long ago, and trite, and as if it had happened to somebody else. The realization had shown her how much her priorities had changed in such a short time.

On the night of her first practice, Kate had been sore and tired and wanting to do nothing but sit. She had gotten Joey to sleep and, with a sigh, plopped herself down on a log, her back against one of the Grandfathers. Ash sat across from her. They remained in silence for a while, now and again taking a jab at the fire to keep it alive. Ash pulled out a penny whistle and started to play a haunting, wistful melody, reminding her of the Celtic music her parents had played so often.

"I like your playing, Ash. It sounds so much like the Irish and Scottish music that was always playing at my house."

He looked at her from across the fire, the flames casting an orange glow over his skin, his eyes dark. "I am not surprised, Kate," he answered. "That I am not." He straightened. "And would you like to hear the history of the People of Ruis?" he asked.

Kate had looked at him, dressed in his leather pants with his long, dark hair pooling about his shoulders.

She nodded and he smiled. Then his gaze drifted to the fire and became unfocused.

"Long ago, when Earth was so very young, there lived two peoples: your people and mine."

"Two different races?" she asked.

"Not so very different as that," he replied and paused. "It was as if two different spirits lived amongst one race: those who would use their gifts and those who were Earthbound and unable to perceive their gifts. But the two lived in harmony, nonetheless.

"I presume it to be natural that like would be drawn to like, for that is what happened. Those with the knowledge of their gifts were drawn to one another, and those who were more of the Earth remained with their kind. But still there was harmony, and the two peoples relied upon each other's strengths to enhance the quality of all their lives."

Then Ash paused.

"But it didn't stay that way," Kate guessed.

"Aye, 'tis true, Kate. It did not. Jealousy and fear erupted within the hearts of the Earthbound."

"My people."

Ash glanced up at her. "Your people.

"And they drove your people away?"

"That they did." He glanced at her again, his brow furrowed. "But among your people there were still ones born with the knowledge of their gifts. These people either merged with our people, or they hid their gifts, or…"

"They were persecuted?" Kate asked.

Ash nodded. "Sadly, yes. It is why we thought it best to leave. If the Earthbound could show such cruelty to their own, it was only a matter of time before they came after us."

Ash put another log on the fire and they watched the sparks dance heavenward.

"My people foresaw how it would be," he continued. "So they sent Walkers out to search for a new home. And after long years we found Ruis."

"And you moved to Ruis."

"Aye, we moved to Ruis."

Kate smiled. "So you are a faerie."

Ash blinked. "No, I am a Walker."

She laughed. "No, I mean your people are the faerie-folk of legend. You know—the Irish call them the Tuatha de Danann."

Ash had smiled, then, and made a courtly bow. "I suppose that I am a faerie, then."

* * *

80

"I hear no *kiai*," Ash said, and Kate was instantly back in the present. How long had he been watching her, she wondered?

She lowered her *bokuto* and crossed to where he was standing, holding a towel for her. "Thanks," she said wiping her face. "Good morning."

"Good morning, Kate." Ash squinted at her. "Your eyes. You look tired, Kate. Did you not sleep well?"

Kate sighed. "Actually, no. I keep having the same nightmare over and over, and I just can't get back to sleep after I have it."

Ash stiffened and grabbed her forearm. "A dream?" he asked, scowling. "For how long, and why did you not tell me immediately?"

"Owww." Kate glared at him, and he dropped her arm.

"But why did you not tell me?" he asked again.

"Why should I?" she replied, rubbing the mark left on her arm. "A dream's just a dream. A lot of stuff has happened to me, and it's only natural that I'd be processing all this. It's my problem, not yours."

"And for how long, and what is the nature of this dream?" His voice was gentler, and her anger dissipated.

Kate walked with him back to their camp and rested her *bokuto* against a tree. "About two or three weeks, now. I had it, and then I didn't for a few days, and then I had it again. I keep having it more and more these days." It felt good to be able to talk about it.

"Is this dream always the same?"

"Yes, yes it is."

"And its nature? Will you tell me, Kate, of what you are dreaming?"

She gathered her thoughts. "Well, I wake up and go outside, and I see both you and Joey lying dead on the ground. Then I see my father with a bloody sword. But it's really Straif, and he kills me, too, says something about how the Prophecy is no more. And I just let him kill me. I just stand there. I don't even try to fight. It's pretty horrible, actually."

81

Ash pulled Kate into an embrace and hugged her, hard. Kate, too stunned to pull away, stood still, listening to his heartbeat.

"This is no dream, Kate. This is a sending," he said. "But how?"

Ash released her, smoothing her hair from her face. "Your father! Kate, I am sorry. I should have thought of that."

"Of what?" Kate asked, dazed.

"When Straif took on your father's persona—Oh! And he touched you as well! He was able to establish a connection with you, directly."

"But, what does this all mean?"

"It means that Straif has hired a dream-maker to send you these images through the link that he has with you. Here, sit, Kate."

Ash guided her to a log. He went and got her a bottle of water and waited for her to drink.

Squatting in front of her, Ash gripped Kate's hands, watching her face. "Straif has three objectives. One, he wants you to feel fear, so that when he does find us, you will be afraid. Two, he is training you to not fight in defense of yourself. Three, he is trying to see where we are hiding."

Kate's eyes widened, but she did not interrupt.

"It is all right, Kate. Now that I know, I shall go to Ruis and get what I need to block the sending from reaching you."

"But I've been dreaming it for a while now. What if Straif's plan has worked?"

Ash smiled and addressed each of the issues. "Do not worry, Kate. Fear is natural, and a little fear keeps you focused. You know this already. And of course you will fight. You will not allow someone to kill you without fighting. It is not a part of your nature. I see the doubt in your face, but I have trained with you. I know how you think. You can trust this. It is truth."

Ash leaned back onto his heels. "Of the third? Has he discovered where we are? That I do not know. Tell me exactly what you saw in your dream, because what you saw, he will see."

Kate grew pale and her mouth went dry. "Then he has seen everything! Oh Ash! I've brought him to us!"

"Be calm, Kate. Tell me *exactly* what you see in your dream."

Kate closed her eyes. "I wake up and look around the home that we have made. Then I go outside and I see you—dead—and I see Joey—dead—and I see Straif as my father."

"Do you look around at the landscape?"

"Noooo," she answered slowly, "not really. Just that tree over there." She pointed to a redwood about fifty paces from where they sat on the edge of the meadow that they had turned into a practice field.

"Ahhhhh, so that will be his portal," Ash answered softly.

Kate felt frozen. "When?"

"It will be when it will be, Kate. I honestly do not know. But soon, I think." Ash looked at her and gave her hand a squeeze. "Thank you, Kate for sharing these things with me. I must think on this."

Kate watched him walk over to the tree that Straif would use to get to them. For a long time, he stood in front of it, as still as a statue.

From within their lean-to, she heard shout and, with a sigh, she rose to fetch Joey from his pen.

* * *

Ash returned as Kate was preparing breakfast. He quietly took the bowl of oatmeal she offered and sat beside the fire pit near Joey, who was studying a caterpillar crawling across his blanket.

"Don't you even *think* about putting that thing into your mouth!" Kate told Joey, as he started to reach for it. She intercepted his grasp and put a bowl of oatmeal in his hand and a spoon in the other. "Have at it, buddy," she told him as she plopped down beside her charge and took a spoonful of cereal from her own bowl.

"I know what we will do now, Kate," Ash said.

She glanced at him expectantly. He radiated confidence.

"Today, we will work with my sword so that you will become familiar with its balance."

Her mouth too full of cereal, she gave him a 'thumbs up' sign. Kate had been waiting for this day.

"And when you are comfortable with the sword," Ash continued, "I will hunt for my Kinsmen. It is time."

Kate found it difficult to swallow. She took a sip of water to clear her throat, but Ash continued before she could object.

"I cannot give you anything to stop the sending from coming to you. I am sorry, but if the dream does not come through to you, then he will know that we know what he is doing. And that would surely force him to hasten his attack."

Kate looked at Joey who was intently gazing at Ash. She scooped him up into her lap. "Well," she said. "This is what it's been about all along, hasn't it? Training me to watch over Joey so that you can find your Kinsmen."

"Aye, Kate, that it has. I will aid you in the washing up, and we will begin."

With Joey strapped onto Ash's back, the two set off to the training field. Only a few weeks ago the grass had been at her waist, Kate thought as she looked at the bare and trampled earth.

"We sure have trained hard here," she commented.

Ash glanced at her with a smile, "Aye, that we have."

They walked in silence to the middle of the meadow and stopped.

Ash pulled the sword that was fastened at his waist. "This is TinneHolm," he announced. "I will perform the purification ritual, and then you will perform it. That is how we will begin."

Kate watched as he slid the sword back into his belt and then wrapped the scabbard's cord through to keep it secure. "Ash? How can you be sure that Straif will attack with a sword, anyway? What if we've been wasting our time? Why wouldn't he just use a gun or something?"

Ash paused to look at her. "A sword it will be. He comes to assassinate a prince."

"But why is that any different?"

"There is a code that we live by," he explained. "Straif will not deviate from it."

"But how can you be so sure?"

"I can. Come, Kate, we waste time."

Kate folded her arms and watched as Ash performed *Harai Tachi*, the purification draw. Despite the added weight and awkwardness of an infant in a backpack, his movements were fluid and graceful. In a split second, the sword was in his hand, the silver glistening bright in the sun. His left hand came to meet the sword as it swept up into position. He stepped forward and made a cut, then brought the sword, blade parallel to the ground, slowly in an arc in front of him as his left hand again returned to grasp the lacquered scabbard. With a twisting motion, the blade was returned to its home.

"Wow," Kate breathed.

"Now it is your turn," Ash said with a smile. He pulled the sword from his belt and handed it to Kate. "Always keep your thumb over the *tsuba* like this," he warned. "You do not wish this blade to become unsheathed uninvited."

Kate took the sword with excitement. She had handled dulled practice swords before. But never anything like the one she now held in her hands. Kate could feel its age. She felt she was holding a piece of ancient history, very beautiful and very deadly.

"The name 'TinneHolm,'" Ash said quietly, "means 'best in the fight.'"

"TinneHolm," Kate repeated, studying the sword. With her thumb carefully on the *tsuba*, Kate raised the sword in front of her so that she could get a better look at the intricate patterns of runes and whorls carved into the scabbard, squinting to make sense of the patterns. The runes, she realized, must be the sword's name. She wondered if the same runes were on the blade itself.

Without thinking, she slowly slid the sword out of its casing. It was heavier than she had supposed.

She was right. The same runes were on the blade. The reflected sun dazzled her eyes.

"TinneHolm," she repeated in a whisper. She felt mesmerized by the sword's beauty, and honored that she was actually holding such an ancient piece of craftsmanship.

Ash spoke, but Kate did not listen. He sounded very far away.

"TinneHolm," she said for a third time. The sun was so bright on the metal that she could barely read the runes any more. It hurt her eyes.

With a gasp, Kate realized that it was not the sun's reflection after all that was so bright, but rather the sword itself. As it became still brighter she felt, for the first time in her life, true terror. The illumination, the power, the runes, the loss of control all collided in her heart and body.

Kate took a step backward and tried to fling the sword from her, but to her horror, the sword held fast to her right hand.

Her eyes wide with fear, Kate watched her own hand perform the same purification ritual that Ash had done. But instead of it being placed within the scabbard at the end, she watched helplessly as the blade slid lightly over the palm of her left hand. She felt no pain as the blood welled up from the cut, and she was given no chance to think because the sword again moved.

This time the back of the blade pressed against her forehead, and she sank to her knees as her left hand joined her right on the *tsuka*.

When the cool, glowing metal touched her forehead, it was as if a cord had been played, too low for the human ear to hear. Yet the vibration coursed throughout her body, her ears ringing.

Kate felt energy surge through her, and then she heard a chorus of voices, all women, one after another. She suddenly realized that she was hearing names, countless names. And when the last name was spoken, Kate felt compelled to add her own to the list.

She spoke her name. The words rang out clear and strong, and she felt a sense of welcome and of homecoming.

And then all was quiet.

It took Kate several moments to realize that she was in control of her body again.

She looked at Ash and tried to speak, but no words issued forth. Her hands shook, and she would have dropped TinneHolm had not Ash taken it from her and returned it to its scabbard.

Silently, he bound her hand in the towel that she had brought and closed her fist around it.

 Keep your hand like this for a little longer, Kate. It is not a deep cut. It will heal quickly."

With Ash's help, Kate stood and dusted off her knees.

"What just happened here?" she asked.

Ash gazed at Kate for several moments before answering. It felt as if he were seeing her in a whole different light.

"TinneHolm was forged more than one thousand years ago," he replied. "It is one of twenty-one swords that were created for an elite group of highly trained warriors, the Sword Maidens, sworn to protect the great kings of Brendt. Each sword was endowed with a life force of its own, and a Sword Maiden and her sword would form a bond that would last the lifetime of that Maiden. When she died, the sword waited for its next battle ally. Kate, TinneHolm has chosen you to be the next Sword Maiden it will serve."

Kate shook her head. "But it's your sword, Ash. I don't understand."

"Actually, the sword belonged to my mother. I was merely caring for it until it bonded with a warrior. At her death, my mother told me I would find its next partner. And so it seems that I have. You belong to TinneHolm and TinneHolm belongs to you."

"But I'm no warrior. I'm not even from Ruis! Why would it pick me? There must be some mistake."

Ash laughed. "After what you just experienced, how could you doubt this? The sword looks for a certain spirit to be its ally; spirit, rather than skill. This blade is a vessel that contains a thousand years of skill! It does not lack skill. What it lacked was a warrior with a noble heart with which to share its skill."

Kate looked at him blankly.

Ash smiled and put a hand on her shoulder, turning her towards their camp. "Come, Kate, I will show you how to clean your sword. We will practice after you have rested a bit. But, in truth, I am no longer concerned with your training. TinneHolme will teach you far more skill than I will ever possess."

* * *

"I am to leave at dawn, Kate."

Kate looked up from the fire. "What? *Why?*"

"The sooner I find my Kinsmen and Ioho is safe, the better I will feel."

"But I'm not ready for you to go. Not yet!"

"But you are ready, Kate. That you are."

Kate glanced at him and said nothing. She stabbed at the fire with a stick until sparks shot high into the air.

"I will never be gone for more than three days. With luck, I will find my Kinsmen straightaway. If it takes longer, I will still return every three days."

Kate squinted at him through the flames. "Why do you think it will take a long time? Don't you have an idea where they might be?"

Ash ran a hand through his hair, his fingers trailing through the heavy, dark strands. "If our main encampment was ever attacked, then the plan was to go deep into the mountains where we had buried supplies in several places. We would not create a new settlement. We would move from place to place until the danger had passed. That way, no one could locate us, because our position would always be changing. Further, only the highest ranks knew the hiding places of all the supplies. The rest of us knew only two or three. I plan to go to the locations that were entrusted to me. If luck is with me, my

Kinsmen will be there. If I cannot locate them, then it will take additional time for me to track them."

"Why can't we come with you? Now that I have TinneHolme, I can help."

"As long as Ioho remains in this Sanctuary, I can be assured that he will be unharmed. I cannot endanger Ioho by bringing you both with me."

"Then why can't you come back each night?"

Ash sighed and rubbed his face. "Kate, I have thought through the choices that I have. My Kinsmen are also looking for me. I will go to places where messages might have been left for me. I will visit and talk with people. I will leave tomorrow and will return in three days."

It was Kate's turn to sigh. "I just don't think that I'm ready to take care of Joey alone. I'm afraid that Straif will come while you are gone."

"I understand," Ash said quietly. "But I must go, and you must trust me that I know you are prepared."

Kate nodded, but she did not feel prepared. She sat staring at the fire, lost in worry. Ash stood and went into the shelter. She could hear him rummaging among his things. When he returned, he held a leather-bound book in his hands. It was scuffed and worn.

"This is the Book of Phagos. There is a passage I would like to read to you. I remembered it earlier today when you were made sword-bound by TinneHolme."

Ash opened the book and held it close to the fire so he could search for the right passage. When he found it, he tilted the book further. He glanced at her. "This is from the Prophecy that tells of Ioho's coming."

He began. "When Ioho is in need, there will always be another—a maiden with the mane of a lion and the fierceness of a tiger, a Walker from our long ago past, to stand by the One-Who-Brings-Peace. She will be a Sword Maiden, following an ancient tradition, and she will be known as Eaeda, The Shield. And wherever Ioho goes, there too will be His Shield."

Ash closed the book and looked at her. "She is you, Kate. You are Eaeda." A chill went up Kate's spine.

"But it says she would be a Walker. I am definitely not a Walker."

"We do not know that, Kate. When I return, I will test you." He rose and stretched. "In the meantime, I do not doubt that you can care for Ioho."

Kate looked long into the fire. "But I do," she whispered.

* * *

Kate woke suddenly. A shaft of moonlight from the opening fell full in her face. All was still. Out of habit, she glanced over at Joey's sleeping form and gave a half-smile. The savior of Ruis had his thumb in his mouth. She reached over and drew the covers around him, even though it was a warm night.

"What was it," she wondered aloud. "What woke me up? There was no dream." She glanced over at the other mound of bedclothes.

Ash! He wasn't with them. Her mouth went dry and she reached for a knife. Quietly, she slipped out of the tree, and into the night.

At first she didn't see him, but when she did, relief flooded her. He stood on the overlook, tall and still. The moon had turned his long black hair a silver-blue. A breeze toyed with some strands. She marveled how it fell almost to his waist. Only someone as magical-looking as Ash could get away with that, she thought. He was so beautiful.

She meant to go right back in. She knew tomorrow was going to be a rough day, but she stood for some time watching him, wondering what he was thinking, what he was feeling. It must be lonely, she decided, to be a Walker, someone set apart from the rest. Was it lonely?

"We don't have one on Ruis."

She jumped. "Have what?" Her voice sounded loud and harsh. His was soft, like water.

"A moon. We have no moon." He turned toward her. "Look how it changes everything. How all the colors are differing shades of blue." He came closer and lifted a strand of her hair from her shoulder. "Your hair looks almost green." His face wore a soft smile as he glanced at her. Then his expression changed. There was something more. "Kate?"

She didn't know how it happened. In one moment they were standing facing each other. In the next, they were kissing and there was warmth spreading throughout her body. He felt so good! She ran her hands up his strong back, feeling the play of his muscles, liking how their two bodies fit so well together. And his hair! It felt like silk, heavy and soft. It felt the way she had imagined it would. He was perfect. He felt like home.

Ash loosened his grip and held her at arm's length. He gazed at her wonderingly, a surprised smile on his face.

"I…that…Kate." His voice was husky, and he cleared his throat. "I…I did not mean for that to happen, Kate."

Kate's smile mirrored Ash's. "It wasn't such a bad thing to happen," she replied.

Ash laughed softly and reached out to stroke her face. "This is not the time for me to talk of my feelings for you." He pulled her back into his arms and rested his chin on the top of her head. "But I will tell you this. I have watched you over the weeks, Kate. I have come to admire your courage and your spirit. I have come to enjoy your company." He paused. "And now," he continued, "I no longer wish to be without your company. Ever."

Kate looked up at him, and he kissed her again. She tightened her grip about his waist and melted into the feelings.

Ash took a deep breath and stood back so he could see her face. "Kate, when Ioho is safe with my Kinsmen, there will be time, if you are willing, for me to court you."

Kate laughed at the old fashioned phrase and kissed him. "Do you need to ask?"

91

His smile seemed to light his whole face, and he hugged her close again. "There is so much I want to show you, Kate, so many places, so many worlds to explore." He laughed. "With you as my reward, I will find my Kinsmen in less than a day!"

Kate looked up at him with the moonlight shining on his beautiful face. She burned his image into her memory, knowing that this moment would be one she would always treasure. Her heart sank when she realized he would be gone at dawn.

Chapter 11 – Sword Maiden

Kate was in a good mood. Ash was expected home that afternoon, and the past two days had proven uneventful. And Ash had been very hopeful when he left that this was the last trip he would need to take. He had had a fairly good idea as to his Kinsmen's whereabouts.

This was the fourth time that she and Joey had been left alone as Ash searched Ruis for his Kinsmen. She was much more relaxed about it and, although she preferred being with Ash for more reasons than one, she enjoyed her special time with Joey.

They had developed a little routine, and the three days went by quickly. This morning, because of the heat, Kate had changed the pattern. Unusual for Northern California, it had not cooled down the night before, and the two of them woke up feeling hot. So, after breakfast, Kate took Joey down to the little creek below the meadow and they splashed together in the water.

"Look how big you're getting," she said to him as he stood in the water, hanging onto her fingers. "Soon, you'll be running all over the place." She shook her fingers and he sat down with a plop and a giggle. She poured water over his head and laughed when his eyes rounded with surprise. She poured water over her own head, enjoying the rush of coolness. It felt good having her hair long and loose, and the fact that her tank top and shorts were soaked made no difference in the heat.

They played a little longer, and then Kate toweled them both off, put Joey in the backpack, and began her daily inspection of the perimeter of their campsite, as Ash had instructed.

Ash. A smile played upon her lips. On each of the prior trips he had come back with a small gift for her. She had accused him of courting her, and he had gone slightly pink. She liked that she could make this serious warrior go slightly pink. She liked how he was slowly taking her into his confidence and trust. And she liked being in his arms.

Kate wiped the sweat from her face and gazed up at the sun.

"It looks like lunch time," she said to Joey. Her stomach growled. "Now it *feels* like lunch time." And she spun around in a circle, making Joey laugh. "Let's go, baby prince."

* * *

After lunch, Kate put Joey down for his nap. She was tempted to just let him lie in the open because of the heat, but then decided that although it was hotter in the lean-to, it was also sheltered from the sun. She watched Joey fight sleep and decided to sing to him softly until he drifted into slumber. She watched him for a little longer, then stood, leaned down to stroke his damp curls, and exited the shelter to clean up their dishes.

Something had made her look up, and she gasped as the adrenalin surged throughout her body. There he was, his blond hair tied back in a braid, his cape swirling in the wake of his movements. Straif's stride was purposeful, relentless. His left hand was on his scabbard, his face an expressionless mask.

Keeping her eyes upon him, Kate slowly stood, wiping her hands on her shorts. She reached for TinneHolm, which she had been keeping next to her at all times.

He stopped a few paces away from her, scrutinizing her with one eyebrow raised. "And so, it is to be like that, is it?" he asked as he unfastened his cape and let it fall where he stood. She was surprised by how much he sounded like Ash.

And then, like lightening, he drew his sword as she drew hers, and they faced each other, bodies tensed and ready. When she saw they were in the same stance, the stance of nothingness, it made her realize that he would know all the sword moves and countermoves that she had learned. She swallowed.

As if reading her mind, Straif laughed. "Do not be so afraid, Maiden. I shall give you the opportunity to show me what my brother has been teaching you. I would not want all of his hard work to be for naught."

Kate drew in her breath and focused her intent on the battle at hand. All of her years of gymnastic training and competition had given her the ability to shut out distractions. She knew her body, how it moved, what it could do. And she consoled herself that she had TinneHolm, her Sword Ally, clenched tightly within her grip. Kate was as ready as she was ever going to be, so she made the first move. He dodged her cut, but just barely. The look on his face told her she had surprised him, and it gave her heart.

They circled, still facing one another. Suddenly, Straif lunged and she deflected his blow, countering with one of her own before he danced out of range. She nicked his wrist and he looked surprised again. She looked at her forearm and saw that he had nicked her as well. She steeled herself for more cuts.

"You are either very, very good or very, very lucky. Which is it?" he asked. And he ran at her. She met his *kurai tachi* with one of her own, realizing how much stronger he was. But she used his force against him in a move she did not know she knew, and nicked him again before she darted out of range.

As she readied for the next clash, it suddenly occurred to her that TinneHolm had performed that last move. *How does the sword work with me?* she wondered. As she continued to fight, she got her answer.

It was simple. If she could defend herself, the sword was quiet. If she could not, it came to her aid. She supposed that is what Ash had meant when he said that the sword would teach her, because, with it as her ally, she was not being seriously wounded, even though Straif had drawn blood on more than one occasion.

His sword was so sharp that she had not felt many of the cuts, but she could see the lines of red multiplying on her wrists and forearms as they fought. When she glanced down at her legs and saw the amount of blood that was trickling down towards her tennis shoes, she fervently wished she had put on blue jeans that morning for extra protection.

Straif noticed her glance, and he smiled maliciously. "You do realize that all those cuts will weaken you, do you not, Maiden? Perhaps I should hasten your ending." And he rushed her, but this time, with a loud *kiai*, she did a back tuck, landing out of range.

Straif smiled. "Now that was really very pretty! Would you like for me to show you some of my tricks?" His face became blurry as his features rearranged themselves into those of her father as he lunged at her.

Kate gasped, but maintained her guard and countered.

Straif backed out of range. His features changed again and he became Ash.

Kate froze.

Straif laughed deep in his throat. "There is always one face," he explained, "that imprisons an opponent's actions. I believe I have found that face for you."

"That face is too good for you!" Kate shouted. "You could never be like Ash! Never!"

"Then this will be the last face you will see before you die. Consider it a gift." And he rushed at her, intending to dispatch her.

She met him, their swords clashing and she held him, *tsuba* to *tsuba*. But it wouldn't be long. He was so much stronger!

It was at that moment that TinneHolm flared into life. Although Kate had been connected to it throughout the battle, it was different this time. It was as if TinneHolm somehow knew that Straif was no longer toying with her and was fighting in earnest. The sword suddenly twisted as Kate clung to it, and it sneaked through Straif's guard, managing to cut him deeply, but not deeply enough.

His features once again his own, Straif backed away, a line of crimson forming across his chest, his eyes on the glowing sword that Kate was holding. For a moment, all that could be heard was their heavy breathing.

Straif wiped his face on his sleeve.

"So, it is TinneHolm that you wield. I had not noticed. And it looks like it has claimed its new master." His smile grew sly. "Well, then, Sword Maiden, this will be much more amusing." And he took a stance of readiness.

Kate glanced at TinneHolm, watching it glow and shimmer in her grip. She shook the sweat from her eyes, tightened her grip, and took a forward leaning stance as she moved TinneHolm into the *mugamae* position. Her instincts shouted that all would be lost if she ever broke contact with the sword.

The battle began in earnest now. Straif rushed in, meaning to finish her. But TinneHolm was fighting now, and she almost laughed at how rapidly she was gaining the upper hand. One thousand years of experience could not be defeated. Joy surged through her as she followed her sword's lead, and watched Straif's expression change from arrogance to fear.

TinneHolm began to move faster, and Kate could barely keep up with the sword's maneuvers. Straif's breathing became more labored, his eyes more fearful. She knew he would not last much longer. Without realizing it, she was grinning as she marveled at the deadly grace of her sword. *Her sword* !

When TinneHolm knocked Straif to the ground, she knew he was about to die. But Straif had rearranged his features into Ash's once more.

"No!" she shouted, and she pulled back. She knew it was Straif and not Ash lying beneath her blade, but she could not kill him. She just could not. The sword lost its glow and lay still in her hands.

Seeing his chance, Straif used his sword to knock TinneHolm off-target with such force that it fell from her grip. And before she could react, he had run her through with his blade.

Straif rose above her, as Kate sank to her knees and then onto her back as he pinned her to the ground. He stared down at her white face, as she lay gasping. "As I said, Maiden," he smirked, "there is always one face." He cocked an eyebrow. "Still, it has been quite some time since I have known fear like that, I must confess to you.

And so," he said, as he drew his sword out of her and raised it over his head, "out of respect, I will end this quickly. Good-bye, Maiden."

Straif brought his arms down to deliver his final cut, then stopped, his face suddenly pale, his eyes wide. He looked at Kate, who was gripping something in her hands, and then down at the glowing sword embedded in his chest. His own sword dropped harmlessly to the ground.

Slowly, as his features again became his own, Straif collapsed on top of Kate and was still.

Trapped where she lay, Kate looked up at the blue, blue sky. "I am a Sword Maiden," she whispered. "I will not let you kill my king."

Then she closed her eyes and knew no more.

* * *

From someplace warm and dark Kate drifted back into consciousness. She took a breath and grimaced at the pain. Slowly opening her eyes, she found herself staring at the canvas ceiling of a large tent. Shadows flickered on the walls.

"Kate?" a familiar voice asked quietly.

She turned her head and found herself staring into Ash's eyes. He lay beside her. Joy rippled through her and she smiled slowly. He looked pale and weak. Kate frowned.

"We are in a healing tent, and we are not to move," Ash said weakly.

"Why?" Her voice was a mere whisper.

"I gave half my life's blood to you, Kate. You were that close to death." He smiled at her look of concern. "I will be fine in a few days' time. You," Ash's gaze became tender. "You will take a little longer, and then you will be fine as well."

"Joey?"

"He is missing his Sword Maiden."

Kate smiled weakly.

She swallowed slowly, then, whispered with great difficulty. "Tell him…not going anywhere."

Ash smiled gently giving her hand a squeeze. "Aye, that I will, Kate. Rest now."

They lay in silence, hand in hand, looking at one another.

"You carry half my life's blood, Kate," Ash murmured. "You are now a Walker."

THE END

C. B. WILLIAMS

About the Author

C.B. Williams lives on five acres in the Northern California redwoods with her husband, son, two dogs, five cats and the wild things that share their space with her.

When she's not writing or being a manuscript midwife, you can find her either painting, playing or adventuring.

C.B. has a black belt in Kashima Shin Ryu, where she learned that a black belt is just the very beginning.

Now available: The Place Between Worlds, Book Two of the Walkers Trilogy (The link is on her website.)

Coming in 2013: The Shield, Book Three of the Walkers
Enjoying the Walkers Trilogy? C.B. loves to hear from her readers, so feel free to contact her.

Website: www.2inspire.us   Email: cbw@2inspire.us